~*~

FIRST PLACE, Reader Views Literary Awards

CHOICE AWARD WINNER, Rebecca's Reads

FINALIST, First Horizon, Hoffer Awards

FINALIST, Readers' Favorite Book Awards

"Riveting and action-packed...a dramatic fiction about violence, betrayal and life lived in the shadows...It takes some brilliance in writing for an author to bring together two worlds, and make them work in a way that offers up a Buddhist lesson on the soul of a man... You don't want to put it down!"
S. Marie Vernon, PACIFIC BOOK REVIEW

"It reminds me of a good roller coaster. Not too long, with enough twists and turns to leave you breathless and an ending that makes you proclaim 'Wow! What a ride!'"
Liz Evans, AMAZON REVIEWS

"There is a lyrical beauty in the tale as Jarret discovers himself and his soul. I loved this book."
Jack Magnus, READERS' FAVORITE REVIEWS

"The story gripped me from the very first page...Very powerful and well-written...A great read."
Barbara Goldie, THE KINDLE BOOK REVIEWS

"I could not put it down...a quick, thrilling read. Excellent!"
Savannah Mae, REBECCA'S READS, CHOICE AWARD WINNER

~*~

SHaDOW GAME

by

Darryl Sollerh

SHaDOW GAME

Night

A dark room.

A ticking clock.

A man in a chair.

His eyes are closed, but he's not asleep. Never asleep.

He is sitting straight-backed in the stillness, absorbed in a motionless waltz with insomnia, awaiting the moment when all his preparations will lead to an inescapable apogee.

But in this moment, in this room, as in so many other rooms and cities before it, he is biding his time in the gathering hush before dawn, allowing only the faint buzz of his alarm to finally break its spell.

Jarret stirs, slowly opening his eyes to the darkness as if awakening to all he knows to be true. He checks his watch and rises, dressed in a craftsman's plain coveralls. His hair's cut short, his fifty-some body lean and seasoned, his every move refined to an elegant economy of function.

As the first rays of dawn glow through cracks in the shutters, he pulls on a pair of surgical latex gloves, pours himself a glass of water and drinks it thoroughly.

He then turns to the room's undisturbed twin bed where a formal waiter's uniform has been neatly laid out, from its demur black bow tie to its patent-leather shoes. He dons it meticulously, piece by piece, pulling on its black pants and crisp, white shirt, finishing with a cream-colored waist jacket, taking care to smooth away any creases.

Last, he lifts up his trench coat, checking the heft in one of its pockets, then slides the water glass into the other pocket and slips out of the room like a ghost.

The Mark

A gray, wet Paris morning awaits him as he steps from his rundown hotel and heads on his way.

He passes rows of sidewalk cafes just opening for the day, their owners glancing skyward, concerned by the dark, gathering clouds.

He moves on, unnoticed, locating a public trash bin into which he discreetly discards the water glass and surgical gloves, then turns down a wide avenue to make his way through the chilly morning to an ornate hotel, rising like a twelve-story throne above a lush park.

Bypassing its gilded entrance, he continues down a side street, angling around to the hotel's backside, where an unmarked door admits the staff.

Checking to see if he's been followed, he moves to blend in with the other workers arriving for their daily shift, entering a backstage, cigarette-clouded world of waiters stealing mid-service smokes, and housekeepers adjusting their maid costumes designed with lacy, school-girl details to reassure the wealthy clientele of their infinitely superior status.

Jarret moves on through a large, bustling kitchen, turning out immaculately plated soufflés and croissants, and continues on to a small, dank change room smelling of cloying aftershaves and sweat.

Taking off his trench coat, he pauses, withdrawing briefly back into himself. He then takes out the object in question from its pocket and moves on, focused and precise.

Minutes later, a twelfth floor service elevator door opens, delivering Jarret, now pushing a linen-draped breakfast cart onto a long, carpeted hallway of penthouse suites.

Ahead, two bodyguards note his progress, puffing themselves up more out of boredom than concern as Jarret rolls the cart toward them like a supplication, decorated with a red rose and two silver chafing domes.

Whoa there, Jacque.

Jarret looks up, feigning confusion as the sandy haired one, a former Rugby player, pats him down while the dark-haired one, who looks to be an ex-military man, inspects the cart, checking under its linen drapes and then lifting back its two chafing domes to reveal a creamy eggs Benedict, served with fresh, red raspberries.

Satisfied, military man knocks on the suite's door, and a moment later it opens, prompting Rugby to motion Jarret in.

Jarret enters submissively, maneuvering the cart to find yet another bodyguard pointing to a grand bay window.

Over there.

Jarret obeys, positioning the cart to take advantage of the Parisian views as the bodyguard moves off.

Sir? Your breakfast's here…Mr. Petrovich?

In his absence, Jarret lifts away one of the silver chafing domes to retrieve a polymer gun taped to the interior, and its complimentary silencer taped inside the other, deftly assembling them as the bodyguard returns.

You got the wrong room, pal.

Petrovich, a heavy man, pads out from his bedroom a moment later, toweling off from his shower, to find Jarret standing there.

Hey. Idiot. I didn't order any—

But he stops short, shocked by the sudden sight of his bodyguard lying on the carpet. He blanches and pivots to escape, but then freezes when he sees Jarret calmly training the small gun at his head.

As Petrovich's eyes storm, a small spffft marks his moment.

Out in the hallway, Rugby and military man hear a faint thump. They check with each other, uncertain what it could be. When only silence follows, Rugby knocks, waits and then knocks again. He then tries the door, but it's locked.

Glancing at the military man, they take out their guns as military man steps back and charges the suite's door, busting it open.

They rush in to find the two bodies face down on the white carpet, pooling halos of blood. As Rugby rushes to check Petrovich's pulse, military man takes up the hunt, soon joined by Rugby.

They make their way through the large suite, checking each room like commandos, making their inevitable way back to the grand master bedroom.

Positioning themselves just outside its door, they share a silent countdown and then charge in and fan out to discover that the suite is empty.

Momentarily confused, military man's eyes dart, quickly noting that the French doors leading out to the terrace are ajar. So he advances on them, getting ready for a decisive confrontation.

But when he bursts out onto the terrace, whipping his gun from side to side, he discovers that it's empty, too.

He quickly speculates that his prey must have escaped via a neighboring terrace and rushes back inside.

He crossed over to another terrace!

Rugby follows military man out of the suite, high-stepping over the two bodies to get back to the hallway, where they take up strategic positions—Rugby by the stairs, military man by elevator.

A few, long seconds tick by, but nothing happens.

The bodyguards exchange a look, worried their prey may be escaping by another way. But then another suite's door opens and a waiter starts backing his way out into the hall…

Rugby and military man charge at him, driving him to the floor and jamming a gun into his face only to realize he's not Jarret.

Recalculating, Rugby rushes for the elevator and bangs at the button as military man angles for the stairwell.

Jarret, hiding behind a small wall separating the hotel's terraces, peeks back into view, climbs skillfully down to a terrace one floor below, and enters another master suite through its French doors.

As a shower hisses in the background, he strips off the waiter's uniform, down to his jumper, and stuffs it under the bed. Then he hears,

You hungry, dear?

He quickly hides behind the bedroom door as a man enters and leans into the steamy bathroom to call to his wife.

Want me to order you something?

With the man momentarily preoccupied, Jarret dodges out of the bedroom and moves through the suite, escaping back out into the eleventh floor's hallway, where he heads for a service elevator, swipes its cardreader with a stolen key card, and boards.

In the lobby, Rugby rushes off the elevator, elbowing his way through the offended guests to get a better view, just as military man bangs out of the stairwell, gun in hand, adrenalized.

As alarmed guests gasp and duck for cover, military man and Rugby head for the Staff Only door, where they rough-arm their way through the dressing rooms and into the kitchen, accosting any waiter they can find, causing a commotion.

While the backstage staff hurry to see what's happening, Jarret's service elevator arrives in the midst of the chaos, allowing him to navigate anonymously through the confusion to collect his trench coat and slip back out onto the street unnoticed.

As he quickly blends back into the busy morning foot traffic, a thunder clap announces a storm surge, sending a downpour just as Rugby and military man spill out the staff's entrance into the deluge.

They look around desperately but Jarret is already gone, lost to them in the morning rush and rain.

Walking the vintage streets, allowing the rain to wash over him like a baptism, he arrives at a Metro entrance. Glancing behind him as a precaution, he then joins in with the crush of Parisians descending to the trains.

Halfway down the stairs, hemmed in by the squeeze and din of the other commuters, he doesn't hear the man rushing down from behind, forcing his way forward, bumping people as he passes and bangs into Jarret, causing him to slip, fall, and crack the back of his head on the stairs behind him.

In an instant, a darkness envelops him, drawing him up into an immense universe of incomprehensible expanse, silence and peace. Momentarily suspended in its womb, he feels himself floating, weightless, only to then feel himself exhaled out in all directions like a rush of light, diffusing him into a singularity, a oneness with all around him, until...

Until the far-off patter of rapid-fire French begins to disturb the stillness and peace, calling from the back of his awareness like a distant meteor shower, but then growing louder, nearer, becoming more like a shower of prickly needles, then like shards of glass, then like jagged rocks cascading, thundering into an avalanche, shattering the stillness and peace as it bears down on him, crushing him once more into his body where he wakes up to the blinding storm of the moment to see a ring of alarmed French faces leering down at him.

He instinctively struggles to his feet, pushing back their offers of assistance and pressing on his way, ignoring their protests, escaping the scene as quickly as he can.

Later that night, awake on an international night flight, he gingerly touches the swelling at the back of his head with his fingertips, finding a swollen, stinging lump digging into his skull like a blade. As he tries to reposition himself so as not to accidentally bump his wound on the seat's headrest, a stewardess passes. He asks for a glass of water.

She nods and moves off, trailing a fading swirl of misty colors, flowing with yellows and reds that deepen into blues and purples before disappearing into the darkness of the cabin.

Jarret stares after her, incredulous.

He blinks, rubs his eyes and draws in a deep breath, trying to halt the effect. He then looks up again, only to see pale peach and crimson hues glowing faintly from the tops of the other passengers' heads seated in front of him.

Alarmed, he looks down again and closes his eyes for the rest of the flight.

Berlin

A shaking shudder and screech, followed by a cabin-rattling roar awakens him back to the present as the plane touches down, and he opens his eyes to see the morning's light glaring in through its cabin windows.

Cautiously, he glances around at the other passengers, more than a little relieved to find that the colors are gone and that order has been restored.

Another night.
Another room.
Another ticking clock.

The next day he's in an unmarked van, holed-up in its cargo bay, eyeing a GPS device.

As its little red star displays his target's position, Jarret opens a nondescript black case beside him and expertly assembles a handmade assassin's rifle and muzzle and then checks the view from the van's side-cabin window to see a well-heeled restaurant with a valet out front.

His GPS begins to beep more quickly, and he takes up the rifle, spying through its scope to watch as a man pulls up to the restaurant in a red Lamborghini, accompanied by his super-model dinner date. As the Valet hurries around to open the Lamborghini's door, Jarret locates the man's head in his crosshairs and is just about to pull the trigger when a wash of colors smear his vision, glowing up mists of orange and crimsons around the man.

Jarret startles back, blinking, trying to quickly restore his vision. He then peers back through his scope but more colors seem to glow off the man and now from his date, too, as they fold arms to head to the restaurant's door.

As Jarret strains to take the shot, the man drops his valet ticket. As he stoops to pick it up, it allows Jarret a moment to adjust so that when the man straightens back up, he rises right into Jarret's crosshairs.

Click.

The man reacts in sudden shock and drops to the sidewalk.

As his date kneels to see what's wrong, Jarret sets aside the rifle, quickly slides back into the van's driver seat and pulls calmly away into traffic, leaving a scene of growing panic in his wake.

He turns onto another street, now out of view of the restaurant, and continues on, testing his eyes, shaken.

Home

A dark airplane.

A back seat.

A troubled mind.

Jarret keeps his head down, his eyes closed, his attention turned inward, trying to reenter his secret world of silence.

He draws in a deep breath and waits, fully expecting the maternal stillness to open to him once more, to welcome him back into herself like a mother welcoming her child home, offering him her eternal protection, hush, and sanctuary, only to discover she's gone. In her absence, a vacant silence remains. A void.

As his flight skids down onto the runway at LAX in the afternoon, he finally opens his eyes again from the restless shadows of his journey.

Avoiding eye contact, he retrieves his carry-on bag from the overhead compartment and joins in the slow moving queue off the plane.

Just ahead, a little girl, curious about him, looks back to appraise him, finding neither fault nor merit as she eyes him, unafraid. He notes her interest, but as her unwavering gaze lingers on him, he begins to feel exposed and puts on a pair of dark glasses.

After what feels like several lifetimes in customs, he finally steps out into the hum and exhaust-scented breeze of the airport to flag down a cab. Climbing in, he gives his directions without looking at the cabby, then sits back, his journey nearly complete, only to soon find his progress slowed yet again by Los Angeles' freeway traffic.

As the cab creeps along, bumper to bumper, the cabby, sensing his moment, tells his well-rehearsed tale of hard luck and family misfortune, lobbying for a bigger tip. But he soon gives up in the face of his passenger's stoic silence.

With a rust-orange sun sinking behind them in the west, the cab finally makes its way into Los Feliz, taking the last few turns up a winding, narrow road to Jarret's vintage address—an aging, 1940's four-plex perched on a steep hillside.

He pays the cabby with barely a glance, and, shouldering his bag, begins the long climb up the cracked cement stairs to his once-elegant one bedroom.

Halfway up, a Golden Retriever bounds down to greet him, a furry flurry of ecstatic tail-wagging and slobber. Warming to the canine's excitement, he doesn't see Gloria, an attractive, black, athletic forties as she steps from her nearby apartment in a flimsy, revealing kimono.

Hey, Stranger. Where ya been hidin?

As her pooch continues its fuss, he reluctantly looks up at her, wary he'll see the colors.

Hey.

Maybe you should get a bitch. Who knows, they just might mate.

She smiles slyly, not the bashful type.

He manages a non-specific semi-smile, relieved to not see any colors around her, and continues on to his door.

Gloria watches after him, more perplexed than offended as he disappears into his apartment.

Even with his blinds drawn, the sunset's golden rays spill in through cracks, gilding his austere rooms in glowing strips of light, revealing little more than a coffee table, a chair, and a small TV.

Glancing around, he unshoulders his bag and, having nothing else to do, sits at the solitary table, looking very much like a man who has no idea what comes next.

The next morning he's in Sunland, seated in a back booth of an air-conditioned diner off the highway, shielded from the growing glare of the new day.

A cup of coffee rests on the worn-Formica tabletop in front of him. A black gym bag sags at his feet. His eyes are down, his focus inward.

Testing himself, he slowly raises his sight-line to take in the other customers scattered around the diner.

They look normal, colorless, content in their morning routines, just as he had hoped.

He eases, relieved to find his world returned to normal until a mom drags her little boy into the diner, yanking him roughly forward, slapping at him to keep him quiet before shoving him into a booth near the cash register. Her boy, maybe six, helpless to defend himself, recoils in fear as she berates him, batting at him some more for good measure.

Jarret sobers, his attention focused on the boy, as Rafa, an earring'd twenties with a taste for tattoos, bangs into the diner toting a gym bag identical to Jarret's.

He looks around as if he owns the joint, interrupting a waitress as she tries to take an order.

When she points out Jarret in the back, Rafa squints, finally seeing him, and starts over, motioning that his eyes haven't adjusted to the light.

Jarret seems to prepare himself as Rafa drops the bag by Jarret's and slides into the booth.

Where do you find these places, brah? The diner time forgot.

Jarret checks his watch, readying to leave.

So?

So?

How'd it go?

Rafa waits, hungry for details as Jarret eyes him without answering, then moves to go.

Wait. I didn't mean ta —

Rafa reaches over to touch Jarret's arm, to delay him, but then sees the look in Jarret's eyes and withdraws.

I'm just interested, okay?

Can't help you.

Then who will? All I need is one. Just one gig, and I'm in.

In?

In like people know I'm for real.

Jarret eyes him again.

I'm not a manager, Rafa.

Might as well be, brah. Ya get all the gigs!

Rafa sobers, realizing he's crossed the line.

That didn't come out right. I'm just—ready, ya know?

Jarret picks up his check.

If you don't believe me, check this out!

Rafa fumbles for a paper in his breast pocket and unfolds it onto the table, displaying a shooting range target pock-marked with bullet holes.

From three hundred yards, brah!

As he is admiring his own handiwork, it takes Rafa a moment to notice Jarret's icy gaze.

Put. That. Away.

Rafa folds it back into his pocket, more resentful than chastened.

Sorry. I just...

Jarret gets up to go.

All I'm asking is could you put in a word? Could you do that much?

A disturbance draws Jarret's attention, and he looks up front again to see the mother harshly scolding her boy. Now he retrieves the gym bag Rafa brought with him, gestures for Rafa to stay put, and starts for the front, pretending not to notice the mother and boy as he arrives at the cash register.

But as the mother starts up her berating again, swatting at her cowering boy with one hand, while preventing his escape with the other, Jarret's eyes storm. He places a twenty by his check, turns, steps over to the mother, grabs her by the collar–shocking her–and lifts her halfway out of the booth to glare into her stunned face.

Stop it. Understand? Stop it, or I will.

As his eyes burn into hers, she lets go of her son, who cringes away confused as Jarret shunts his mother back into the booth and strides out.

As he climbs into his Buick, an ancient wave of memory crashes over him, driving him down into the raging, suffocating waters of the past, sweeping him along with its impossible power, drowning him in its black depths until he's somehow able to grab onto the car's steering wheel and hang on long enough to pull himself from its undertow, finally breaching once more the surface of the present, gasping for air, exhausted but alive.

A road wind buffets his face as he speeds through San Gabriel, caressing and calming him. He's finally able to draw in a deep breath and let it out, restoring order.

Another half hour's drive finds him in Arcadia, pulling into an aging, low-rent self-storage facility. He navigates his way through the weathered buildings and parks outside his unit. Soon he's walking down an empty, dimly lit corridor past rows of bolted storage units, carrying the black gym bag.

Moments later, locating an elegantly hidden key he leaves on site, he opens a small storage space to dig through piles of cardboard boxes, some loosely packed with old travel magazines but most empty, to unearth an unmarked box buried in the back.

Checking again to make sure he's alone, he slides out that certain box and opens it to reveal deep stacks of cash packets.

He eyes his life savings dispassionately, unzips the gym bag revealing fifty thousand in neatly-crimped packets and starts transferring them into the storage box, until he hears a creak.

Instantly hiding his work, he turns to see an old Security Guard leashing to two Dobermans, leaning in.

Hey, there. How do?

Jarret smiles casually, feigning ease, only to sober as he sees the colors glowing up around the Security Guard's head and body.

The Guard arches a brow, concerned by the look on Jarret's face.

Gee, didn't mean to give ya a start.

No, everything's…okay. And you?
Oh, can't complain. But then, wouldn't matter if I did.
The Security Guard pats his dogs.
Ain't that right, fellas? Anyway, we just sayin' hello.
Thanks.
Jarret watches him move off, the colors trailing and fading into the shadows.

A dark, doctor's office.
A neurological examination.
A light glaring into his pupils.

Follow my finger.
Jarret does as Dr. Alvarez pans it from side to side, finally stopping and stepping over to flip on the room's light.
You on any meds, legal or otherwise?
No.
Any headaches, nausea, vomiting, dizziness?
No.
Alvarez considers.
I'd like to schedule a CAT-scan to see if—
No.
The doctor peers over the top of his reading glasses.
Unless we can get a better sense of what's—
No. Thanks.
In that case, I want you to take it really easy the next few weeks, okay? And if you see any more colors, you'll call me. All right?

Fifteen minutes later, Jarret is back on the freeway, returning to Los Feliz.
As the long afternoon leans into evening, his phone rings. He glances at the caller's ID–unknown–and clicks to answer, but waits for the caller to identify first.
It's your one-and-only, lover. All back safe and sound, are we?
Everything's taken care of.
Of course it is. It always is with you. Which is why we need to talk.
Can't.
Can't?
I'm taking some time off.

And nobody deserves to more than you do, handsome. But it'll have to wait until after we talk.

If this is about a—

Ya know where to find me, baby.

She clicks off.

His jaw tightens. He's tempted to ignore her demand but then decides it's better to have this out now, in person, so he changes freeway lanes and angles back to North Hollywood.

Twenty minutes later, he's cruising down Riverside Drive, pulling into the small, crumbling parking lot of an old fabric store.

He climbs from the Buick and looks around, thinking this will be his last time here. He then walks around to the front, where a sun-bleached Se Hablo Espanol sign hangs at an angle on the shop's glass door. He enters, jiggling a bell.

Long, messy aisles are piled high with fabric spools, creating corridors crammed with colors, textures and patterns. Jarret glances around and then spots Helen, a sultry sixties with a subversive Southern charm, fingering fabrics near the back with a seasoned touch.

As he approaches, she senses his arrival without looking up.

I'm lookin for somethin girly for my niece. Somethin ta bring out the female in her for once.

Hello, Helen.

She turns to drape a lilac swatch across her cleavage, modeling it for him.

Ain't no use bein a woman if ya gonna hide it, honey.

He waits, wanting to get down to business.

What, we beyond cleavage now?

He endures.

Looks like ya lost a few pounds, poor baby.

Travel will do that.

Try bein' a women. We can put on five pounds just thinkin' 'bout chocolate.

As she fingers more fabrics.

Men have so many advantages it could make your pussy spin.

She holds up another swatch to his cheek this time, appraising his coloring.

You're definitely a Winter, honey. Now my niece, she's a Spring. It's all in the colors. That's the secret, sugar.

If this is about a job, Helen, I won't be available for a while. Fact, I might not be available at all.

She pauses to eye him a beat and then gets back to her fabrics.

Nobody deserves a vacation more than you do, handsome. But business is business.

You're not hearing me, Helen.

She turns to face him.

And you're not hearin' me, darlin'. We're talkin' triple your usual quote for two days work.

He holds his ground.

Did I mention I made all the arrangements myself?

I am done, Helen.

Done? My, my. So what, exactly, am I supposed ta do now? Give it ta Rafa? Give a boy a man's work?

She searches his eyes knowingly.

Only reason I came here was so that I could tell you in person.

She considers it before responding.

Well, Tiger, there's done, and there's all done. So how bout ya postpone your all done long enough ta do this one for me?

He remains silent.

As a favor? ...For all the years?

It's not what you think.

It's not what ya think, either, honey. Truth be told, I kinda got my titties in a ringer on this one. So if there was anythin' ya ever liked about me, this would be the time ta show it.

As I said, I can't.

I promised them the best, honey. And that means you. And as far as your little surprise announcement goes, this was supposed ta be my last one, too. So you're not the only one ready for retirement.

It's his turn to be surprised.

That's right, lover. Flip me over cause I'm crispy done. Or at least I was supposed ta be. Folks I'm dealin' with, they ain't the kind ta let a girl in-the-know go, if ya see what I mean?

He consider it.

In that case, I could help you go away.

Only one way ya can help me now, sweetie, is do what I need ya ta do.

...I'm sorry, Helen.

She seems to go into herself, then smirks.

Famous last words, baby.

She moves on, fingering more fabrics as if he wasn't there anymore. So he turns and leaves.

So much for long goodbyes tumbles through his mind as he climbs back into his Buick and drives away.

In his apartment, seated at his table, he glances at a travel magazine featuring exotic getaways. As he considers a photo of an isolated beach along an empty coastline, someone knocks on his door.

Reacting instinctively, he moves quickly to position himself behind the door.

It's me, Gloria. ...Hello?

He cracks open his door to find Gloria holding a pot as her golden retriever, Chincha, nudges his nose excitedly at the narrow opening.

Hey.

Hey.

Thought you could use a home cooked meal.

He opens the door to allow her in, and Chincha charges in, only a little less eager to enter than his owner.

Looks like he kinda has a thing for you.

Gloria moves to his kitchen, noting its virtually unused state as she puts the pot on the stove to heat it.

You keep any dishware?

Jarret opens a cabinet to reveal disposable plastic ware.

And I thought I was afraid of commitment.

This stuff's easier.

Not on the planet, it isn't. But then, by the looks of things, I'd say ya keep a pretty small footprint.

I don't like a lot of stuff.

That go for people, too?

As he considers how to answer, she grins.

Don't have to explain to me. It's why I got Chincha.

As he tries to look casual, she senses his unease.

You cool with this?

Sure.

You sure?

It's just that...I'm going to be leaving soon.

Leave this apartment?

Los Angeles.

She takes a moment to ride out her disappointment.

Then I guess we better eat up, before you're gone, right?

It's...

She waits, all ears.

It's just...something I need to do.

She considers, finding her center again.

I hear ya. Hell, maybe I need to go someplace else, too.

Later that night, Jarret is seated in his chair, staring into the dark when another knock compels his attention.

He gets up, thinking it might be Gloria again, even hoping it is, until he peeks out to see Helen standing at his door.

Surprised and suspicious, he hesitates, considering what to do as she knocks again. He finally opens his door, and they eye each other a moment as if coming to terms. Then she says:

Do ya want me on my knees, lover? Is that it? Cause I'll get down on my knees. I'll do anythin' ya want ta do. Or you can do anythin' ya want ta with me. Just do this one thing for me. Okay?

How'd you find me?

You'd be surprised what a girl can do when her life depends on it.

He eyes her.

Ya gonna leave me standin' out here like some jilted lover?

He opens his door so that she can step inside. As she does, she notes his monk-like décor, seeing for the first time where and how he lives, after all these years.

What do you want?

Ta get away from all this...ruin.

Ruin?

Think I'm jokin? I'm not, baby. Trust me.

She looks around, taking in his existence.

Funny seein us like this. Me comin' over here at all hours of the night like some love-sick girl, beggin' the boy who dumped her ta make love ta her one last time.

Why are you here, Helen?

The thing is, sugar, if this job don't get done, and in the time and way it needs ta get done, some boys are gonna come callin' on yours truly, and not cause they like me.

What are you talking about?

I'm talkin' about what we've done for a livin, sugar. The kinda people ya meet in our line of work. Long story short, there ain't no turnin' back now. Not for me.

Meaning what, exactly?

Meanin' if I say sorry boys, that thing we talked about, I can't do that now like we agreed, ya think they just gonna shrug and take their business elsewhere? No. There's a price for bein' privy ta the things we're privy ta.

So why's this time different from all the other times?

Cause of who these boys are. Cause of how much they don't like quitters. And cause I told 'em you were the best.

So leave, Helen. Go away somewhere. Tonight. You don't need the work.

Don't work like that, darlin'. Not for me. Not for you.

I'll help you.

Only way ya can help me now, lover, is ta do this one, last gig. Take ya two days, tops. And I seein ta everythin. All ya gotta do is show up, do what you do best, then we'll both be done. For good.

He considers as she eyes him, her gaze betraying a desperation he's never seen in them before.

Do this for me, and I'll do anythin' ya want, babe. Anythin'. ...Stay. Go. Anythin'.

As he stands there, still on the verge of saying no, she starts sinking to her knees in sexual supplication, but he catches her, getting filled with a confused mix of colliding emotions, and raises her back up.

Trembling, she lays her head on his chest. He allows it, conflicted, as she whispers:

Your flight leaves tonight.

A long night flight.

A dark cabin.

A last gig.

Jarret's awake in the dark as the other passengers sleep. An Indonesian stewardess moves past his seat. Testing his vision, he looks after her, checking for the colors…but seeing none, he eases back to rest, reassured.

The sweet scent of a tropical breeze mixed with diesel exhaust brushes over him as he steps out of the airport terminal into the bright day to find a row of rickshaws and drivers competing for his business.

One driver's white hair and persistent manner convinces him, and he soon finds himself speeding through a lush countryside, past verdant farms, rice fields and villages blending Asian and Indian influences like savory spices.

Arriving in Jakarta, he's quickly engulfed in its routine mania, replete with blaring traffic horns and police whistles as pedestrians, rickshaws, cars, motorcycles and buses all compete for space and advantage. His rickshaw joins into the fray, accelerating and breaking sharply as it maneuvers its jerky way to a rundown hotel on a sketchy side street.

Looking around, his driver then eyes Jarret as if there must be some mistake—a white man coming to stay here?

But Jarret sidesteps the question by paying the driver and heads into the seedy digs without a moment's hesitation.

Entering his room, he finds the requisite squeaky bed, chair, TV and shallow closet.

Leaning into it, he looks up to see a removable, attic panel.

With the chair positioned in the closet's door jam, he steps up onto it and lifts away the attic panel. Then he feels around until he locates a rucksack, and carefully pulls it down.

Back at the bed, he unzips the rucksack to find a disposable cell phone, a digital camera and a black case, which could be mistaken for a trumpeter's case, until he takes it out and opens it. Inside, neatly tucked into foam bedding, he eyes a disassembled sniper's rifle, with a box of 7.62mm cartridges. Taking them out, he inspects a few cartridges carefully, checking for any imperfections in their casings before putting them back.

He then takes out the rifle parts, deftly assembling the lean, skeletal construction by screwing its barrel to the shoulder rest and firing mechanism, then fitting on its scope and silencer.

Checking its sight-lines and metallurgic integrity, he finally draws it up into shooting position and slowly pulls on the trigger until it clicks.

Satisfied, he adroitly disassembles it again, fitting the pieces back into their foam bedding like a puzzle and then closes the case with a snap.

He takes a moment for himself as if snapping something in him back into place. He then slides the case back into the rucksack.

Turning his attention to the camera, he powers it on and shuffles through a series of stored photos to see various angles of his mark—a gregarious looking man in his forties greeting an adoring throng of villagers and farmers. Toggling ahead, he finds snapshots of recent newspaper headlines identifying his prey as Bahru, an opposition candidate running for President against one General Matak, a short, implacable-looking man in his sixties with an apparent fondness for army fatigues and dark sunglasses.

Photo after photo reveal the extent of Bahru's political popularity at crowded rallies, as well as the violent, tear gas confrontations they seem to ignite.

He eyes them coolly, committing Bahru's face to memory, interested only to complete his work here and retire into the anonymity of a man finally—finally finished with it all.

He then removes the camera's memory card, takes out a disposable lighter, lights it and drops it into an ashtray to let the flames complete their work.

Last, he flips open the cell phone, turns it on, and texts: OK.

He then shoulders the rucksack, composes himself a moment, then heads back out into the late afternoon, carrying the camera like a tourist.

Stepping out onto the narrow, busy street, he finds himself engulfed again by the humid air, now filling with the smells of steaming rice, tongue-scalding chilies, pungent garlic and clove cigarettes, mixing with hints of piss, sewage, sweat and mold, punctuated by the wafts of dank perfumes and frenzied colognes trailing various passersby.

He moves off into the crowds, keeping his eyes low as he angles into the narrow streets of a local marketplace, crammed with merchant booths that seem to create a rambling, distended city unto themselves.

A bazaar of infinite variety awaits, stocked with everything from T-shirts and textiles to tourist trinkets and postcards, from bogus iPhones and Chinese electronics to burning hot fish and chips, and from chili-fried peppers to sweet, cooling fruits. Here and there he notes posters bearing the likeness of General Matak, meant, when printed, to impress, but now graffiti'd over with scrawls of Freedom Now!, Dictator and Murderer.

Winding his way through the ever-unfolding narrow streets of the marketplace, he arrives at a public square, flanked by weather-tarnished office buildings where a group of young volunteers are busy pasting up their own posters and placards of Bahru, while others erect a small stage and microphon'd podium for their hero's rally tomorrow morning.

Taking pictures like a tourist, he first determines his angles, east and west being the key, by noting the setting sun's position in the sky.

With the podium conveniently to the west, he turns to survey the rooftops to the east in search of a suitable sniper's nest.

An aging, six story office building becomes the obvious choice, putting tomorrow morning's sun squarely at his back—an ideal alignment—because it will blind any who might look to discover his position or try to track his escape.

Using his camera's zoom to get a closer look, he sees a useful array of air-conditioning units and air ducts populating its rooftop.

Freedom talk tomorrow. You come?

Jarret turns, taken off-guard, to find a young man with a yellow headband beaming at him with a big, bright smile, pressing a flier at Jarret.

You take many pictures tomorrow, okay?

The young man again urges the flier at Jarret, insisting he take it with a warm, gregarious nod.

See you tomorrow at ten, sir!

Jarret accepts the flier, but offers only a curt, non-committal nod in return before receding back into the activity of the square.

He then enters the office building in question, passing through an empty lobby to climb its six stories of cement stairs.

With each new flight, he passes a floor busy with textile manufacturing, cellphone sales, jewelry making and bicycle repair. Reaching the fifth floor, he locates a Roof Access door, which leads to a narrow, unlit set of ascending stairs.

With the turn of a knob, he steps out onto the roof, now six stories above the square to note how well the air-conditioning units and air ducts offer him cover, yet leave him a clear, unobstructed view to the podium below.

Checking around some more, he notes with concern a seven story building rising just to the east of his sniper's perch–effectively behind him–and only separated by a narrow alleyway running between the two buildings.

But as he looks it over, he discovers its top floor windows have been boarded over in lieu of glass. Add to which, the air ducts on his present rooftop would likely block any clear views of the podium if he were on its rooftop, eliminating it as a candidate for his perch. So he refocuses on his current position, and makes his way forward, towards the roof's western edge to identify which of the ducts is best positioned for his purposes. Finding one, he kneels beside it.

Checking his sight-lines, not only does he have a clear shot at the podium, he's also able to survey a wide swath of the square below.

Satisfied, he glances around once more, then hides the rucksack inside the air duct's vent, and withdraws.

As the sun sinks into afternoon, he makes his way back into the marketplace. It has grown humid with the day's heat, but even more so from the thousand pots of steaming rice and pungent fish fries.

He knows better than to try them with a Westerner's tongue, and moves on, past a cacophony of calls for his business, to locate a fruit cart owned and operated by a street-savvy, teenage proprietor displaying piles of red melons, mustard-colored horse mangoes, purple Java plums and light green Malay apples.

Instantly sensing a potential customer, the youth fans the relentless flies from his fruit.

Good fruit for you, sir?

Is it fresh?

All fresh today, sir!

Jarret indicates he'll have a bowl, and the youth deftly chops him up a blend of mango, banana and apple.

My name Daksa.

Do you have a knife you could sell me, Daksa?

A knife?

Twenty dollars American?

Daksa's eyes widen, then quickly narrow as he shifts into entrepreneurial mode, quickly exchanging Jarret's bowl of fruit and his extra knife for Jarret's American cash.

You come back, Okay? I have plenty fruit, and more knife, too!

Jarret nods and moves off, angling back towards the public square, eating the fruit, observing the volunteers and noting the square's exit points, taking time to familiarize himself with its layout.

As the afternoon arcs towards evening, he hears raised, upset voices, followed by cries for help and then police sirens. He turns to see a police truck race up, screech to a stop, and unleash a pack of vicious, baton-wielding officers, led by their fanatical Sergeant, a forties man who seems eager for blood.

The police quickly fan out, beating the Bahru volunteers brave enough, or foolish enough, to resist while another gang of officers tear down all the posters, placards and bunting.

As the locals look on enraged but intimidated, Jarret can see the fear, tumult and helplessness burning in their eyes. And it triggers something in him, something old and overwhelming, buried deep inside, yet immediate and alive, and now burning to life on the faces of those around him.

He turns back to the square to see the police continuing their roundup, running down their victims to beat them with metal-tipped batons. Jarret glances up at his sniper's perch, now a moot point, and quickly retreats, disappearing back into the maze of avenues and corridors of the marketplace, escaping the square and the emotions tearing at the faces around him.

Weaving back through the oncomers seeking a better view of the square, he moves to the marketplace where even the distant cries for help blend into the din of the daily business, leaving much of the marketplace blithely oblivious to what is happening only a few blocks away.

Taking one last turn, he finds himself moving down a sumptuous corridor of hanging, jewel-toned silk textiles, shimmering in hues of turquoise, amethyst, ruby reds and topaz yellows, emerald greens and royal blues, undulating delicately in a light, balmy breeze, creating a mesmerizing, dreamlike world apart.

As he passes through it, he begins to hear the sounds of laughter accented by the ooohs and aaahs of a small, unseen audience. As he brushes past the last draping silk, he exits the corridor to discover a small crowd pressing in around a Wayang puppet play, framed in a small stage, fitted into a corner of the marketplace.

On its stage, shadows of kings, queens, paupers and demons move briskly about, enacting their ancient tales in silhouette on a back-lit cotton screen.

Jarret slows, curious, and moves to get a better view, discovering a lithe, thin man in his seventies, the Dalang, looking as if he is in a trance as he animates the flat puppets from behind the stage, giving each a voice and destiny, weaving their stories to the delight of the crowd with the help of candles and mirrors.

Moving around to the front to view the play, he suddenly hears the soaring, pure-toned coo of a wooden flute accompanying the action. He looks to find its source, but can't as it is blocked by others. So he moves again as a gong reverberates, and he sees through a parting of the audience's heads a beautiful Malaysian woman, maybe thirty, seated at the foot of the stage, surrounded by a gong, a flute and djembe drum.

He moves again to get a better view of her, taking in her long black hair, mocha skin and deep-set eyes as she plays, absorbed in her music like a lover.

Thunderstruck by her serene focus, he stares, unable to look away.

As if sensing his attention, she raises her eyes just enough to share a fleeting glance with him before withdrawing again into her music.

Unable to turn from her, he begins to see faint hues of yellow and pastel pinks glow around her, radiating gently, creating a soft halo of light.

Sobering, he rubs his eyes, trying to halt the effect and then eyes her again, only to see oranges, crimsons and purples emanating from those around him.

As his vision fills with the colors emanating from everyone around him, he is brought back to his senses and he quickly moves off.

A moment later he's navigating the marketplace's byzantine streets, escaping, keeping his gaze low as he tries to maneuver his way back to his hotel, buffeted by waves of color flowing from everyone he passes.

He presses forward, feeling attacked and betrayed, looking ahead just enough to maintain his direction until the colors so cloud his vision that he's forced to step aside and wait them out.

He draws in deep breaths and blinks repeatedly, trying to restore order and control.

Slowly, by degrees, the colors begin to fade, allowing him to continue on even though his vision remains blurred.

As he moves forward, he senses someone is observing him; yet knowing better than to look, he proceeds on his way, passing several more merchant stands before suddenly changing directions and darting behind a trinket stand to steal a look behind him.

He sees a shadowy figure briefly step forward to look around, only to abruptly retreat again, determined not to be discovered.

Jarret waits, his eyes peeled, his vision restored enough for him to have seen the shadowed figure, but not enough to have made out his features.

With the shadowy figure now gone, Jarret cautiously moves on, repeatedly checking behind him as he makes his way back to his hotel.

Jarret steps back into his hotel room and locks the door and then moves to the bathroom to splash some cold faucet-water onto his eyes and face, seeking a moment's self-assessment in the rusty mirror.

As his eyes meet themselves in the mirror–his vision nearly back to normal–his cell phone rings. He takes it out, checks the caller ID, and then clicks it on without speaking.

That you, baby?

There's a problem with the meet.

I heard, hun, but I wanted ya ta know it's bein' taken care of as we speak.

Meaning?

Meanin we'll have ta reschedule ta Thursday, but rest assured, it will take place.

Jarret's face tenses, his patience already spent.

But the good news is our employer agreed ta double your fee on account of the delay.

Jarret could care less.

Any more delays, I'm out.

Understood, sugar.

She clicks off.

Jarret slides the phone back into his pocket and eyes himself in the mirror again, feeling himself approaching an inner end point, the cliff he always knew was out there, now at hand, beckoning him, inviting him to take that one, last step, that one, last release into...

He catches himself, pulling himself back to the moment. He returns to sit in the hotel room's solitary chair, repeating his routine like a mantra, trying to withdraw once more into that secret place of silence.

Yet even though his eyes are closed, and his routine intact, all he finds inside him is an empty space, a vacant silence, a void–his peace replaced by the slow-passing pace of the minutes, now counting down to Thursday.

And he's still seated in the chair as the first rays of dawn seek out the slits in the room's shutters, piercing this temporary sanctum with intense beams of bracing sunlight. Jarret opens his eyes with concern, faced with an unplanned, unaccounted-for day.

Minutes later, he steps warily out into the street, testing his vision first on inanimate objects, then on the passersby, checking for any signs of last night's color-clouds. But everything looks to be back to normal with the world, and everyone in it consumed by their own affairs.

So he moves off, reentering the marketplace and its narrow avenues to pass vendors setting out their wares for the day, from leafy vegetables smelling of soil to marble-eyed fish stacked in piles, still wet and sea-scented.

Turning a corner, he again finds himself at Daksa's fruit stand.

Everything fresh?

Everything always fresh, Mister!

So Jarret indicates he'll have a bowl, and Daksa enthusiastically chops and slices him a bowl of mango mixed with jack fruit, papaya and pineapple, which he proudly presents to Jarret, eager to please.

Jarret nods, noting Daksa's enthusiasm, pays him and then moves off, angling again for the public square, sensing the somber mood in the merchants as he draws closer to see torn Bahru posters and placards littering the space, and yesterday's podium toppled and smashed.

He then hears the scratchy bark of a man speaking adamantly into a bullhorn in Bahasa, somewhere nearby. His first instinct is to avoid the hubbub, but he catches himself, reconsiders, and angles back toward the strident, tinny voice.

Searching the marketplace, he finally discovers its source, namely the young man with the yellow headband and big smile from yesterday, now standing on the hood of a produce truck, holding the bullhorn in one hand and a picture of Bahru in the other as he exhorts the gathering crowd.

Soon, his listeners are chanting *Bahru, Bahru, Bahru,* pumping their fists in a sign of unity and defiance.

As Jarret looks around, he catches sight of an obscured man in sunglasses, not chanting, but who appears to have been looking at Jarret, only to dodge away and disappear the moment Jarret's eyes find him.

Jarret tries to maneuver in his direction, to pursue the man, but his efforts are thwarted by the chanting crowd.

And it is then that he sees Lia again, looking even more mesmerizing than before, chanting along with the others.

Still trying to pursue the man, Jarret presses forward, but to no avail. He's long gone. So Jarret's gaze returns to Lia, drawn back to her as if by gravity, becoming ever more conscious of her effortless power over him, until the wail of an approaching police siren stings the air, sending a shock wave through the marketplace.

The young man with the yellow headband jumps down from the truck and takes off as the crowd scrambles to disperse, creating instant bottlenecks in the narrow streets as yet more police sirens wail up, signaling the onset of another melee like yesterday's.

Jarret finds himself caught up in the surging currents of panic as groups of merchants and shoppers try to escape in various directions, only to be bullied back by the police who herd them into each other as their fellow officers pursue the young man in the yellow headband, hell-bent on making an example of him.

Jarret then sees the same vicious Sergeant from yesterday stride arrogantly into the midst of the cowering crowd, drunk with his power.

As several of the Sergeant's officers move to coral the crowd, the true object of their interest, the young man with the yellow headband scampers past on the next street over, knocking over produce bins and trinket displays in a desperate bid to slow the pack of baton-wielding officers pursuing him.

In the chaos, Jarret escapes into a doorway as the chase continues, cutting off any obvious avenues of exit. So Jarret retreats into a door jam to hide away. As he does, he sees Lia hiding behind in a merchant's booth, biding her time, too.

Once more, he finds himself staring at her, despite the riot around them. And just as before, Lia seems to sense Jarret's attention and looks over.

She holds his gaze for a moment, but then hurries away as another pass-by of the young man shifts circumstances again, opening an escape route.

As the Sergeant shouts after his men, demanding they catch him, Jarret takes off after Lia and soon finds himself sharing her escape.

As they move back into the marketplace, now punctuated by the cries of the police and the crowd, another rush of officers chasing the young man causes Jarret to lose track of Lia. But given his own need to escape, he hurries on, exiting the marketplace and retreating back into the anonymous safety of his hotel room.

That evening, as he sits in the waning light of the day enduring the humidity under a ceiling fan which rotates above him to little effect, he clicks on the TV to find a state-run news station denigrating Bahru, with images of rioting and violence and then contrasting them with adoring footage of General Matak waving to his supporters as they toss flowers at him.

Jarret shuts off the TV, allowing the room to darken again and then checks his cell phone for messages and, finding none, puts it aside.

With nothing to do but wait, he sits back into the chair and closes his eyes. Soon he sees Lia in his mind's eye, hiding in the marketplace. He then relives their escape, moving through the melee together, only to lose her in the rush and panic.

And suddenly he finds himself as if transported back to the marketplace, looking for her, driven to find her in the chaos, confounded by her effect on him. But then everything shifts again, and he's eating a bowl fruit as Daksa looks on, his face gaunt from poverty and overwork.

So Jarret retreats, trying to get away from Daksa and from the stifling crowd pressing in around him. Turning, he sees now a parade of impoverished beggars and children lurching past, causing him to try to turn away again, only to have everything shift yet again, replacing the parade with an abrupt stillness, leaving him suddenly alone in the twilight.

Everyone is gone, inexplicably disappeared, leaving him abandoned in the marketplace now darkening into night.

He looks around warily, confused as the beat, jangle and rattle of a procession marching his way emerges from the silence, first at a distance, but then coming nearer, angling toward him, filling the night with its hypnotic rhythms as if coming from every direction.

He spins around but cannot find its source in the shadows as the insistent beat of the procession draws closer and louder and closer and louder until…

He awakens to feel his heart racing, his pulse pounding, his forehead beading sweat.

Feeling feverish, he gets up and pours himself a glass of water. Drinks it down. Waits. But it doesn't help. His heart's still racing.

So he tries moving back to the chair, but his balance comes unhinged and the world suddenly spins away as if releasing him from gravity, jettisoning him into the void.

He grabs at the wall to hold on as an electric shock jolts through him, weakening him. He eyes the chair, only a few steps away, but now as if across a wide ravine.

Girding himself, he prepares for the leap, only to feel another bolt of lightning.

Hours later, he comes to face down on the floor.

The next morning, as traditional Indonesian music floats on the humid air playing on an unseen radio, he sits on an examination table in a dark office as a spry, seventies female physician shines a light into his pupils.

You watch finger, okay?

Like the last Doc, she moves her finger across his field of vision, watching his eyes track it.

She then steps back to flip on the room lights.

Jarret looks down, concluding this has been yet another waste of time, when a shock of pain suddenly shoots up his leg, jerking his foot involuntarily upward, surprising him, until he raises his eyes to see the Doc holding a rubber-tipped mallet.

Reactions good. Everything seem okay. But you no okay.
Thanks, anyway.
You want come back?
No.

Stepping from the curtained examination room, Jarret moves into the clinic's waiting room, full of mothers clutching whining, sickly children; he then moves on past rows of wiry men with intense stares, draped in spent clothing, wearing shredded shoes, all enduring, persisting, carrying their graves in their eyes unlike Westerners who hide the inevitable at all costs, even from themselves.

Back on the streets, he checks his vision, finds it calm and clear, and starts back for his hotel room, cutting back through the marketplace to save time.

But as he moves through its improvised avenues, he slows, suddenly realizing he's lost his way.

He looks around, starting to feel dizzy again.

Concerned, he gathers himself and presses on, weaving, sidestepping and parrying through the afternoon rush of shoppers, beginning to hear an insistent honking of an unseen car bullying its way forward, even though it doesn't belong on these narrow pathways.

But its honking continues, demanding attention.

So Jarret turns and sees a Peugeot lurching forward, breaking into view, accelerating at any opening, then braking hard and honking at any obstruction.

He then sees a little girl, maybe seven, gripping a little dog to her chest, looking lost and buffeted about by the confused adults reacting to the Peugeot.

As they bump into her in their attempts to clear a path, she loses hold of her puppy, and it slides from her arms to the ground where it starts reacting to all the rushing feet, darting to and fro. As the girl desperately tries to retrieve it, Jarret, anticipating the danger she's now in, starts back towards her just as the Peugeot driver, spotting a new opening, accelerates, gunning right at the girl and her dog.

Stop!

The driver sees the girl and swerves, missing her, but striking her dog before it accelerates away again, causing a ruckus.

As shoppers shout after the Peugeot's driver, the girl screams and drops to her knees in horror, finding her dog lying on its side, shaking spasmodically.

Jarret runs up to find the girl looking up to him for help, her eyes begging for a miracle.

You help, okay? You help!

Jarret stares at her, wanting to explain that he can't help, only to see inflamed colors swirling to life around her.

Please, please. You help, mister, Please!

Jarret looks around him, trying to rally others to her, but as they shy away, it's left to him.

Not knowing what else to do, he kneels and cradles the dog's little head in his hands, trying to appease her tears.

He okay? Please, he okay?

Her dog, trembling uncontrollably now, looks to be on death's door.

Is there a veterinarian near here?

The girl doesn't understand.

A doctor for animals?

The girl shakes her head, tears boiling, streaming.

You help. Okay!

I can't.

Please!

Wanting to look as if he's trying for her sake, he begins to stroke the dog's little head, hoping to somehow calm its spasms. But it continues to shake, unresponsive.

I'm sorry.

As he moves to lay the puppy's head back down, trying to extricate himself, the girl panics.

No, please! We pray! We pray!

Jarret's mind races, and he looks around to discover that he's seeing the colors around every passerby, which only makes him want to escape all the more.

I have to go.

But just as he starts to un-cup the dog's head, he shocks with the sudden jolt of an electrical charge surging through him, twitching down his arms to release into his hands.

Jarret freezes, stunned as the girl reacts to seeing her dog's trembling ease.

Another surge of energy charges through Jarret, sparking down into his hands to discharge into the dog, fluttering its eyes, and causing the girl's face to ignite with hope.

Others begin to take note, gasping at what they see, drawing in still others who press in to see what is happening.

Nearby, Dalang and Lia, carrying home their fresh produce for the day, observe the small but growing crowd blocking the narrow avenue.

At its epicenter, the little girl, sensing her pup's improvement, begs Jarret for more.

Again!

Unable to control it, Jarret feels another jolt ricochet through him, delivering another surge of energy to the dog, causing its trembling to melt away.

More gasps from the locals as the girl cries for still more.

Again!!

Lia, hearing the girl's pleas, moves closer with Dalang to see what has so captivated the crowd.

The onlookers, recognizing the Dalang, make room for him, allowing him and Lia a view of Jarret on his knees by the little girl, looking stunned as another charge vibrates through him, causing the dog's eyes to blink open.

Lia's face fills with a knowing look as Jarret, desperate now to escape, retreats.

Please, more!

I have to go.

Jarret lays the dog's head down and struggles to his feet–his body reeling with strange energies–and pushes his way out of the circle of onlookers to hurry away.

Come back!

As the girl cries after him, another gasp draws her attention back to see her puppy struggle to its feet, shake itself off, then turn to her as if waking from a dream to wag its tail.

All eyes blink wide at the sight, then turn to stare after Jarret, amazed as Lia turns to look knowingly at her father.

Minutes later, Jarret reenters his new room, locks the door and collapses into its solitary chair to hyperventilate.

Slowly calming, he hazards a look at his hands to find them still radiating, pulsing, warm with an unknown power.

He gets up and goes into the bathroom to run water over them, to cool them, trying to assuage the energies still sparking through his body.

He looks up to view himself in the mirror and finds his face couched by a faint glow, undulating with shadows. So he squeezes his eyes shut, and splashes water over his face as his phone rings, startling him, yanking him back to a more familiar reality.

Gathering his wits, he picks the call.

Tell me it's you, handsome.

Something's come up, and I have to leave.

Leave?

I need to go.

He clicks off and moves to pack as his phone rings again. He considers, then reluctantly picks up:

Ya can't do that, darlin'.

I have to. My eyes are... I just have to go, do you understand?

What I understand is that if ya don't get this thing done, it's me that's gonna be the goner. Now do ya understand? So just hang in there for two little more days, handsome. Two, teensy-weensy days.

She clicks off.

He eyes the phone, reeling, then steps back into the bathroom to see his reflection–its earlier glow now dimmed into darkness and shadows.

He moves back to the chair, sits and closes his eyes, on the verge of leaving despite the danger to Helen.

As the night creeps past, he can hear the city's hum, punctuated by a lover's quarrel somewhere down the street, a growling argument between men below his window followed by the pealing laughter of drunk women, their high heels clicking like castanets on the pavement as they stagger home late, spent and satiated, finally ready to concede the night to the crickets.

No sleep comes to Jarret, nor does any rest. And then it's dawn again, rising in the east like a gauntlet, bringing with it neither absolution or answers.

Jarret slowly opens his eyes and looks around cautiously, testing his vision. When he finds that all looks normal, he gets up cautiously and pours himself a glass of water, feeling a fear rising in him from the depths like a leviathan. But he gathers himself and strikes out into the morning, determined to regain his control.

He steps out and checks his vision, finding the world reassuringly normal. So he moves off.

A few blocks more, and he's back in the marketplace's narrow avenues, searching for Daksa's fruit stand. Daksa sees him and calls:

Everything fresh today, Mister!

Jarret turns to see Daksa smiling. As he steps over to him, he hears a lithe voice behind him say:

First time?

Jarret turns to see the Dalang, eyeing him with interest, as Lia, supporting him, looks on, more reserved.

Sorry?

Dalang waits, eyeing him expectantly to see whether Jarret can comprehend his meaning. Jarret feigns unfamiliarity.

Can I help you?

Yes. First time.

Dalang looks to his Lia, confirming his suspicion.

First time for what?

This is Lia, daughter.

Dalang squeezes Lia's arm, indicating she should shake Jarret's hand. So she extends her hand which Jarret, not knowing what else to do, shakes.

How do you do?

Lia's grip is firmer than his.

Hello.

As their moment of recognition hangs in the air, Dalang intercedes.

I am Dalang.

He offers his hand, and Jarret shakes it, playing along.

Hello.

Your name?

Reynolds.

It take time, Reynolds.

What does?

Dalang says something to Lia in Bahasa, which she translates.

To get used to it.

Get used to what?

Dalang again whispers in Bahasa to Lia.

What you see. What happens to you.

I don't understand.

We understand. Which is why my father is offering to speak to you about it.

About what?

Dalang seems to take his denials in their stride.

You come to puppet play tonight, okay? Lia play music. You come, yes?

I'll try.

Dalang beams at him with an intense, irresistible comprehension and then moves off with Lia's assistance.

Jarret watches after them, thrown, confused, momentarily affected only to soon sober back into his infinitely more familiar mindset of distrust–leaving Daksa to wonder what happened as Jarret moves off without buying any fruit.

As he navigates the busy avenues, he passes a collection of windchimes for sale, many with mirrored clappers that, as he pauses to let a shopper pass in front of him, reflect a glancing view of the man with dark sunglasses he saw earlier, now following him again.

So Jarret continues on his way as if unaware, but slows his pace, pausing frequently as if to admire various merchants' wares, allowing the man to come as close as he dares at which point Jarret dodges down a side avenue, hides and looks back to see the man approaching the spot he just occupied.

The man, looking around, sees Jarret spying back at him and takes off.

And Jarret takes off after him, fighting against the crush of shoppers to see the man hurrying down another avenue, escaping.

So Jarret pursues him, weaving his way forward, trying to catch up, but everywhere running into shoppers or sellers who cause Jarret to lose track of the man, forcing Jarret to finally give up.

Minutes later, he's back in his hotel room, quickly collecting his things.

Back on the streets, he takes special care to make sure he's not being followed and then makes his way to an even seedier side street, and locates another tumble-down hotel.

He enters his new room to find another austere cubicle with a chair, a sagging bed and a tiny closet.

He deposits his shoulder bag onto the bed, and, moving the chair away from the door, takes out his phone to call Helen, but then thinks better, and puts it back in his pocket.

A knock on his door galvanizes his attention, and he waits in silence to hear the hotel's manager call him.

Mister Reynolds?

Calculating that it could be a trap, he waits in silence until the manager says something about a receipt.

Jarret cautiously opens the room's door to find the manager, who launches into an explanation for his visit as Jarret eyes him, seeing what looks to be a small, spinning flower-like wheel on the man's brow, emitting hues of lavender and orange, and at the man's throat, a similar wheel hinting faint hues of orange and red.

The manager, reacting to Jarret's off-putting stare, steps back, offended, blurts out something in Bahasa, spins on his heel and marches off.

Jarret stares after him and then shuts and locks the door and sinks into his chair, certain that his condition, his curse, is quickly worsening.

No dreams come. Only the long, sleepless wait of one who has nowhere to rest.

As dawn breaks again through the room's shutters, his eyes open with more certainty, his day already planned and precise.

In the bathroom, he splashes water on his face and then cautiously looks up to check himself in the mirror's reflection, instantly averting his gaze when he sees the faint shadow-hues undulating around his head.

Dressing quickly, pressed by a growing undercurrent of paranoia and panic, he slips out of the room.

In the street he pauses to test his vision before continuing on his way. When all looks normal, he avoids his reflection in a store window and continues on, soon purchasing a tourist's baseball cap and dark sunglasses to obscure his features. But as he moves off from the merchant's booth, he hears someone speaking to him.

I looked for you last night.

Jarret turns to see Lia, standing nearby, not fooled by his disguise.

I...couldn't make it.

Do you have a moment now?

I really have to—

My father thought you might like to see our local Buddhist shrine.
He hesitates. She offers a shrug as if to say, why not?
It's close by.

She indicates a direction, and he succumbs, following her lead as she guides him away from the bustle of the marketplace, the crowds and cars, and out into the tropical hanging greens of an overgrown public park with its strange atmosphere of peace, as if it's a world apart from the pulsing city only steps away.

When she glances back at him, he looks ahead as if focused on their destination and then glances behind, checking to seeing if they're being followed.

They arrive at a large stone Buddha, rising serenely above them, huge and silent, meditating under a robe of moss.
The police will not come in here.
Why not?
Because they do want anybody to see, or know, what they do.
She indicates the Buddha.
So. You like Wayang?
What's that?
Our puppet plays.
They're…new to me.
And what you see, feel, is that also new to you?

She looks at him in a way he feels he can't afford. So he asks a question.
Tell me about Wayang.
They move through the overgrown grounds, finding smaller shrines.
Wayang means shadow because to them, we are the shadows.
Them?
The puppets. They dance in the real world.
Meaning not this world?
This is a world of shadows. They dance in the light.

Jarret allows her explanation to pass without comment. But his eyes betray his doubts.
It's alright if you don't believe. Believing isn't enough, anyway. So why did you come?
Here? Business.
She slows down and eyes him thoughtfully.
Must be difficult.
He pretends not to know what she means.

Business is business.

*I was referring to seeing what you see, but not knowing what you're
seeing, or why.*

He waits, wanting, dreading what she may say next.

The colors round people?

I hit my head is all.

And the little girl's dog?

He tries to hide his surprise.

Even if I hadn't seen it myself, word travels fast here.

*The dog was just a little stunned. And as for the colors, I have a mild
concussion; that's what's causing them.*

Is that what explains it?

Yes.

She seems to accept his explanation, turning her face to enjoy a
breeze, but then comments:

All except for how I would know you're seeing colors.

She looks back at him and then walks on, leading full circle around
the serene, stone Buddha to arrive back where they started.

*I've seen the colors since I was a child. So has my father. But as for
the little dog, that is something different. Something you must learn to
understand.*

Evening falls.

Jarret is sitting in a small, immaculate garden, protected by the
rooms of a home wrapping around him, guarded by a high, stucco wall
that somehow keeps the world at bay even though the marketplace lies just
beyond its doors.

Above him, a turquoise and cobalt sky mixes with fast-fading
oranges, purples and charcoal grays. Around him, the distant sounds of the
marketplace barely compete with an amorous cricket, chirping somewhere
in the yard.

Would you like some tea?

He turns to find Lia offering him a cup. Before he can decline,
Dalang insists:

Have tea.

Jarret accepts, recognizing something in the precision with which
she pours his tea.

Thank you.

Dalang eyes him expectantly, waiting for him to taste it. So Jarret
does, suppressing a wince at its intense, bitter taste.

Dalang then pulls out a pack of clove cigarettes and lights up, forcing Jarret to have to lean to and fro to avoid the pungent, sweet clouds of smoke billowing from Dalang.

You no see play?

No, I had some business I had to take care of.

So you come tonight?

I'll try.

Otherwise, you frog in well forever, yes?

Jarret leans to avoid a cloud of smoke.

A frog?

Jarret looks to Lia for a translation. But she lets her father explain.

When frog in well look up, he see only small part of sky, but think: I see all of sky! He no understand sky much bigger than what he see, yes?

Jarret glances to Lia again for help, but Dalang isn't through.

You are like frog. The well, your mind. But what happen to you now? Much bigger than any mind, yes?

Dalang, eyeing Jarret carefully, takes another deep drag off his clove cigarette.

You come tonight. You see.

See what?

Whole sky.

Jarret glances once more to Lia to find her looking at him, yet not exactly, more as if she's taking in something around him. But then Dalang gets up, signaling the end of their talk.

Lia gets up, too, so Jarret stands, and she walks him out.

Thank you for the tea. And the tour.

Lia nods neutrally and closes the door, leaving him back in the middle of the marketplace's sudden loud din and bustle.

Turning to head for the public square, thinking to retrieve the rifle, he suddenly starts seeing the colors around people again, combining now with hinting outlines of the spinning wheels he saw earlier on his hotel manager's brow and throat.

Goddamnit.

He tries looking away and then looking back. But the colors only seem to glow more vivid. So he steels himself and instead starts back for his hotel, trying to navigate his way through the nightlife while keeping his eyes down.

Bumped by others, he's forced to look up again to better weave his path, finding orange and lavender hues all around him, with passersby glowing yellow or red, with faint spinning flower-like discs from their brows, throats, chests and abdomens.

Goddamnit!

Turning a corner, he sees a familiar, shadowy figure trying on a pair of sunglasses. Jarret slows, recognizing the stocky outline of a young man with earrings, who, he finally realizes, is Rafa.

Jarret is shocked, blinking, squinting to confirm it is indeed Rafa, seeing faint clouds of browns and grays emanating off him like fumes.

At which Jarret moves out of view, hiding behind a vegetable stand to calculate what this must mean. He takes out his phone and dials Helen. The call rings, but she doesn't answer, so he puts it away and looks back to where Rafa was just standing to discover that he's gone.

But it doesn't matter. He's seen all he needs to see. As Jarret takes off again, heading now for the next flight home, he hears:

Hey, brah!

Jarret's face flushes as he slow-turns to see Rafa smirking at him.

Thought that was you, dude! How cool is this?

Rafa moves to bro-handshake him, but Jarret recoils, instinctively checking to see if anybody's watching them.

What are you doing here?

Workin, thanks to you, brah.

What are you talking about?

Like I don't know who put in a good word for me? You can deny it, dude, but I know.

Jarret seethes, moving close to Rafa, gesturing, pretending to be giving him street directions.

I'm not here, and you don't know me, understand?

Oh, for sure, brah.

Don't come near me again.

Jarret then points, as if helping a fellow tourist.

So good luck, and have a nice trip.

Rafa, smirking, half-hardheartedly plays along.

Thanks, man. Same to you.

Jarret moves off, his eyes burning as Rafa watches after him, still smirking.

Jarret takes out his phone and dials Helen again. This time she picks up.

That you, handsome?

What's he doing here?

Who?

"Who"? The boy you better hope comes through for you, because I'm done.

Jarret clicks off.

Leaving the marketplace, he crosses the last few streets back to his hotel. On the way, his phone rings, but he ignores it. Then it buzzes with a text, which he also ignores.

In this hotel room, as he quickly packs his few belongings, wiping off the water-pitcher and taking the glass with him for later disposal, his phone buzzes with yet another text message.

He looks over, thinks about it, and finally takes it up and reads the message:

Client wants a second job done. Had no choice.

Jarret considers. Finally picks up the phone, hesitates, and then places the call.

You sent him here?

What choice did ya leave me, babe?

If he comes near me again, so he help me, Helen—

He what?

He stopped me in the street to say hello.

...That little shit. So help me it won't happen again. Trust me.

Jarret is now ready to leave, but now wants to hear what the Dalang and Lia may have to tell him, to teach him.

Just so we're clear, if the meet doesn't happen, for any reason, I'm done. Understand?

He waits as a silence hangs in the air.

Ya know, handsome, it would be nice if, just once, ya'd say somethin nice ta me 'bout all the years I...

All the years you what?

Kept all of it from ya.

Kept what from me?

It ever occur ta ya some might consider ya a liability, knowin' what ya know 'bout their business?

I don't get involved, and the clients know that.

That what ya think? Well, after ya do this one, it'll all be over anyway. Right?

Jarret waits, noting her peculiar tone. And then she clicks off.

He stands there, looking at the phone. As he plays the conversation back in his head, he hears footfalls making their way down the hallway.

He moves, positioning himself behind the door as the footfalls seem to slow and linger, creaking the floorboards just on the other side of his room's door. Jarret braces, holding himself still until the footfalls move off and fade away at which Jarret repositions himself and gently cracks the door just enough to view the hallway, now empty and quiet. So he eases his door shut again, locks it, and returns to sit in the chair.

Later that night, he awakens, it seems, to find himself alone in the marketplace again. All the booths are open for business, all their wares neatly displayed, but the place is deserted, save for a faint breeze teasing some windchimes in the shadowed twilight.

He looks around, on guard, perplexed as he begins to hear again the hypnotic beat of an unseen djembe drum procession, accompanied by the rhythmic che-che-che of hand-shakers, accented by the bright tings of finger-cymbals in the empty air, growing louder and nearer, surrounding him with its pulsing, mesmerizing syncopation.

As the moon arcs overhead, he turns around and around, searching for the source of the pulsing waves of rhythm closing in on him, ever more insistent, until he turns one last time to see a parade of life-size Wayang puppets coming into view, dancing in a slow-motion display of elongated, sinuous movements and weightless leaps, flashing their fierce, caricatured visages at Jarret, surrounding him, enclosing him with their terrifying elegance and burning eyes, ablaze with impossible power, turning all their attention on him, when an alarm buzzes to life, shocking him back into the silence of his hotel room, already filling with evening's shadows.

He clutches at the chair's armrests, groping his way back into the present.

Needing a distraction, he gets up and turns on the room's TV, its snowy screen soon filling with images of General Matak in his customary army fatigues and sunglasses, accepting the ecstatic cries of his supporters as an excited newscaster narrates. The program then abruptly changes tone to narrate footage of fisticuffs breaking out at a Bahru rally, juxtaposing the two campaigns as if the choice was between order and chaos.

As Jarret watches the TV, he feels his body begin to twitch. Concerned, he returns to sit in the chair as the tremors deepen into convulsions, doubling him over. His muscles tighten, squeezing and twisting themselves like a wet towel. He tries to resist it, to fight the attack, but then everything goes black.

Later, he wakes up on the floor again.

Getting up slowly, struggling to gather himself, he moves to a window, parts the shutters and peers out to see the glow of a late afternoon. He must have been out for most of the day.

In the hallway, stepping out of his room, he pauses to wedge a small piece of paper into his door as he closes it, out of sight, which will stay in place unless the door is opened.

Minutes later, he is standing outside the medical clinic he visited earlier, reconsidering, but instead of going in, he thinks better, and goes in search of Lia.

Weaving his way back through the marketplace, he arrives back at her door, and knocks a couple of times but no one answers.

So he moves off again, not sure what to do, yet relieved to find the world, for the moment, back to normal.

After a few more avenues he finds himself again gazing down that corridor of jewel-toned silk fabrics, undulating in the soft breeze, stretching out before him like a diaphanous dream-portal, beckoning him into itself.

As he stands there, he begins to hear again the familiar ooohs and aaahs of the unseen Wayang audience watching another puppet play. So he walks down the silken tunnel, traveling its flowing length to emerge once more into a small crowd pressed in around the stage to see the puppet-shadows dance in silhouette, telling their tales.

Through a thickening haze of clove cigarette smoke and rising incense trails, Jarret also notes two uniformed policemen standing off to one side, monitoring the scene like birds of prey.

Avoiding them, he searches for a view of Lia, and, finding a spot, settles in to watch her perform, instantly drawn in again by her meditative focus, accompanying the action sometimes with a drum flourish, sometimes by striking notes on her saron or plucking a melody on her sasando, and sometimes by blowing life into her flute.

As he eyes her, becoming transfixed, the colors, pastel hues of peach, yellow and now turquoise begin to faintly glow to life around, as well as a spinning flower-like wheel on her forehead.

This time he doesn't look away, but finds himself looking more carefully at the effects, observing them and searching them for answers.

Within moments, deeper yellows and oranges begin to emanate from those around him, glowing faintly to life like individual signatures.

Yet just as he begins to allow himself to see the colors and not run from them, he feels himself flinch, shot through with a sudden, if now more familiar, bolt of energy.

He braces himself as another electrical storm strikes like lightening inside him, rattling his body.

He quickly lowers himself down to one knee, trying to anchor himself as more jolts rock him. Only a nearby young boy takes note of him as he braces for more, but the adults are too enthralled with the last scenes of the puppet play to notice, charmed by the tale of a lowly-rice-farmer-become-hero, who outwits a vicious demon, and escapes with his princess love to live in safety and happiness.

An enthusiastic burst of applause greets the play's conclusion. As the men, women and children begin to disperse, depositing their donations in a box, they observe Jarret, still down on one knee, doing his best to suppress his body's flinching.

Realizing he best depart before the two policemen take note of him, he tries to climb to his feet, but another jolt of energy rattles him, forcing him back down to one knee. As one of the policemen begins to eye him, Jarret feels a gentle hand fold under his arm and lift him up.

Come.

He opens his eyes to find Lia urging him up, wary, too, of the police. With her help, he rises and moves around the back of the Wayang stage.

Dalang, putting the puppets away in their ceremonial box, looks up as Lia walks Jarret into view, and instantly senses Jarret's condition at which he shoulders his puppet box, stows his candles and mirrors, and joins Lia to take Jarret back to their home.

Minutes later, Jarret finds himself entering their home again. After quickly shutting their front door to hide Jarret from any prying eyes, they lead him through an open courtyard garden and into an austere back room, where they help him to sit on a mat near a large wooden box.

I'll get us some tea.

Dalang sits across from him and un-shoulders his puppet case.

Better?

Yes.

As Jarret breathes easier, he watches how thoughtfully Dalang removes the puppets from the case and then knocks three times on the wooden chest before opening it. He then lays tonight's puppets carefully to rest inside it, like a parent putting to bed his beloved children.

Dalang sees Jarret watching him.

Where they sleep.

Jarret waits for more. So Dalang offers him more, holding up various puppets for introduction.

This is Gotakaca. Boy-Prince.

He lays Gotakaca down in the chest to sleep, then holds up another puppet:

Durno. He warrior. Like Warrior in you. ...And this Shiva, the destroyer.

Dalang lingers on Shiva. Then he lays it to rest to pick up the last puppet:

Semar. He like Monk. Represent oneness of all.

Lia enters with their teas, as Dalang holds up the cotton screen on which the puppet shadows dance.

This Kulit, on which all life dance. One side light, one side shadow. We dance on shadow side.

Lia says something in Bahasa. Jarret waits.

I asked him to say something about what you see.

Jarret looks back to Dalang, who's quickly sobering.

You see light through shadow. Shadow mind. Shadow heart.

Lia looks frustrated, as if she thinks her father should have been more artful. But Dalang is sober, serious, unyielding as his eyes bore into Jarret's.

Will it stop? Can you make it stop?

Dalang snaps the puppet chest closed.

You come with me now?

Now? Where?

Jarret looks to Lia for an explanation, but she has none to offer. As he looks back at Dalang, they hear a loud knock.

Lia shoots a worried look to Dalang as their front door bangs open to reveal two police officers, who Jarret recognizes from earlier, followed by their Sergeant, who Jarret recognizes from the square. Dalang immediately steps out to greet them like old friends.

Sergeant Tre. Welcome. Come in!

Tre takes a quick look around points at Lia and Jarret, then instructs his men in Bahasa.

Take them outside.

As the two officers move to commandeer them, Lia's instinct is to resist, but Jarret shoots her a look of bide your time, so she reconsiders and allows herself to be escorted peaceably out into the marketplace with Jarret.

As they stand there, under guard, they hear Tre scream at Dalang, followed by the sounds face slaps. Lia's jaw tightens, but Jarret subtly pinches her arm, admonishing her not to react.

Tre then strides out to confront Lia, now employing his fluid English.

How many times have I warned you and your father? Do you really think I don't know what you are up to?

Do you think we do not know what you are up to, Sergeant Tre?

Tre slaps Lia, causing an involuntary response in Jarret, which Tre notes with instant interest, and steps over to crowd Jarret.

And you are?

Reynolds.

An American?

Yes.

Your passport, please.

Jarret produces it. Tre inspects it.

What are you doing here, Mr. Reynolds?

Research.

What kind of research?

Puppets. All kinds of puppets.

Tre notes Jarret's intended insult with a slow smirk.

You mean the puppets of terrorists, like her and her father, the Dalang? Who spread nothing but lies about his Excellency, General Matak? Do not let me find you here again, Mr. Reynolds.

He hands back Jarret's passport, and steps over to Lia, smiles, then casually turns, as if to leave, only to suddenly pivot, wield back around and punch her flush in the face, sending her tumbling backwards to the ground.

Jarret ignites, charges at Tre, prompting one of his officers to slam the butt of his gun into the back of Jarret's head. He staggers forward, crumpling to his knees as Tre and his men sneer, move off to climb back into their squad car and drive away.

Lia, bleeding, struggles to her feet and makes her way back inside. Jarret struggles up, too, his head ringing as if a bomb had just detonated inside it. Before him the world seems a wash of glancing colors, glistening like a menagerie. He closes his eyes, grimacing, wanting it to stop, to escape this curse, this beast rising up from deep inside him, coming to devour him, exacting its revenge for a debt unpaid.

Still shaky on his feet, he reenters the home to find Lia pressing a cool towel against Dalang's swollen cheek. Yet the moment Dalang sees Jarret, he looks up more determined than ever.

You come with me now, yes? You come?

Jarret follows Dalang away from the city lights and office buildings and paved streets onto winding dirt roads lined with improvised huts constructed of rusted, corrugated metal panels and salvaged bamboo huts housing the city's life-blood of workers, maids and orderlies, who, after working long, hard hours at their city jobs, return home to all they can afford: these ramshackle dwellings, perched along acrid, urban spillways, smelling of raw sewage and rot.

As Dalang leads on, Jarret keeps a wary eye on the men who watch them from the shadows, following their progress as if assessing their vulnerability.

A police car's siren wails in the night, and Dalang pulls Jarret into a doorway to hide as it races past.

They then press on, turning down a narrow, dark alleyway, and into a dead end. Jarret hesitates, instinctively cautious of a trap, but Dalang beckons him on, and he relents, noting the suspicious looks from a group of men drinking and smoking around a small fire.

Dalang steps up to a small abode, constructed from fading, torn canvas and knocks.

A young mother opens her make-shift door. She's small, with a round face and eyes red from days of crying.

Dalang nods knowingly to her and enters. So Jarret does, too.

Inside, a single candle burns, revealing a sickly boy lying on a ratty mattress on the floor.

The young mother kisses Dalang's hand and then takes Jarret's and kisses his as well, much to his dismay. He turns to Dalang, and finds him waiting expectantly:

What?

Help boy.

How?

Like help dog.

Jarret stares at Dalang, incredulous, but then realizes that the young mother is eyeing him too, full of hope. So he pulls Dalang aside.

What are you doing?

Time you do something, yes?

Like what?

You know.
No, I don't.
Good. Then mind no get in way.
The young mother looks to Dalang.
We have no much time.
To do what?
Help him.
He obviously needs a doctor.
Doctor no can help. Only help come through you now.
But I can't help him!
Help come through you, Reynolds. No from you.

The boy's grandparents step in, a small couple with eyes full of desperate hope, expectation and fear as they take Jarret in and then look to their daughter, wondering if Jarret's helping.

Or you can stay at bottom of well like frog.

Jarret's eyes burn, ready to run, but something makes him hesitate, holds him back, as Dalang, the young mother and her parents all await his decision.

He moves to the boy and kneels, reasoning he'll just cup the boy's head; nothing will happen and then he can leave just as he came, like a ghost.

So he positions himself and takes the boy's head into his hands.

Seconds tick by. Nothing happens.

Jarret waits, seeing no colors, feeling no jolts of energy as the boy seems to sink farther into the grave before him.

He looks up at Dalang, but Dalang indicates he should continue. So he does, feeling as if he's enacting a charade physicians know well, played not for the patient whose moment is near, but for his survivors to feel they have done everything possible.

As he continues to support the boy's head in his hands, more seconds tick by like silent death knells, drawing Jarret's thoughts more and more to why the Dalang would bring him here, promising him truth, only to exploit him, making him party to this pretense, this lie.

Jarret withdraws his hands as if he's done all he could and nods to the young mother in apology, whose face tightens with more tears. He then looks to Dalang, barely concealing his contempt.

As Jarret waits outside, angry, Dalang finally steps out.
Why'd you bring me here?

Dalang eyes him neutrally and then starts off, heading back home.

Jarret, forced to follow if he wants to find his way out of this twisting, improvised shanty-town in the dark, reluctantly walks after him.

They move in silence, Jarret brooding, Dalang betraying no hints of frustration. He simply continues on, unconcerned with Jarret's mood or opinion.

Arriving at the Dalang's home, Dalang opens his door to go in, leaving Jarret standing in the street, waiting for an explanation. But Dalang only turns, nods and starts to close the door, prompting Jarret to reach out and stop him.

That's it?

You rest now.

Rest from what? Nothing happened, except maybe you gave a mother a hell of a false hope!

How do you know?

Jarret shakes his head in disgust.

You call this help? Who, exactly, did you help tonight?

Dalang waits for Jarret to remove his hand, which Jarret finally does, at which Dalang closes his door and then locks it from the inside, accenting what feels like Jarret's summary dismissal with a click of the door's bolt.

Jarret smirks to himself, feeling used, and heads back through the dark marketplace, washing his hands of it all.

Back at his hotel room's door, he kneels before entering to discover that the tiny piece of paper he wedged into the door jam earlier is now lying on the floor.

Readying his knife, he unlocks the door, pushing it open before entering.

When nothing happens, he ventures carefully in, poised for an attack.

Edging forward into its small, dark confines, moonlight splaying faintly in through the cracks in the blinds, he quickly determines it's empty. So he moves onto the bathroom, easing forward, and then kicking the door open find it empty, too.

He flips on the light to look around, finding everything the way he left it, even though he knows it's not.

He takes out his airline ticket, certain now that his itinerary's been compromised, and tears it up. He then collects the water glass, shoulders his rucksack and leaves.

On the streets again, he locates a trash bin and shatters the water glass into it, then moves on, searching for another room even more out of the way.

Finding another hotel, he enters its rundown lobby to find a proprietor's glass booth. He dings its desk bell, drawing a thin, shirtless man with sleep-weary eyes into the booth from an inner, connecting door.

Like a room, please. With a chair.

The man eyes him, noting the late hour.

Fifty dollar, American.

Jarret notes a rate schedule, clearly posted.

That says your room's rent for ten dollars.

You wake me, you pay me.

Jarret enters, checks the closet and bathroom, as well as what lies outside the room's window in case he needs an alternate exit. He then places the rucksack on the bed and moves into its mildewed bathroom to splash some water on his face. As he looks up at himself, much to his consternation, he sees pale yellows and creamy pinks emanating, hovering around him, with faint hints of a flower-wheel spinning between his eyebrows.

He quickly turns away and escapes back into the small room to pace, feeling as if he's witnessing the unraveling of his own mind. Then his phone rings.

He checks the number and clicks onto the call. Then waits.

Hey, handsome.

What is it?

Looks like we're gonna need ta make one, tiny little change.

Meaning?

Helen explains that the "meet" is now on Saturday. For sure Saturday. And that their employer is going to triple his fee to compensate him for the delay. All of which washes over Jarret as if in the abstract.

Dreamless, he spends the night in another slow dance with sleeplessness, allowing only the faint buzz of his alarm to draw him back.

He looks down at his hands. They look as they always have to him, only now the sight of them fills him with dread.

Back in the marketplace, as Daksa hands him a breakfast bowl of fruit with a smile, Jarret hears:

We gotta talk, brah.

He turns to see Rafa behind him, apparently trying to play it low key.

Jarret's eyes storm.

It's like life and death, dude. And it includes you. Which is why I came ta warn ya.

Jarret moves Rafa away from Daksa's booth to a less trafficked corner. Rafa glances around, checking to see if anybody might be spying on them as Jarrte grows impatient.

Warn me about what?

It's a set-up, brah.

A set-up?

You, me, all of it! It's a goddamn set-up to take us both down, dude!

Jarret eyes Rafa, wondering what his angle is.

You have 30 seconds.

I don't even know where to begin.

Twenty-nine seconds.

Okay, okay. Like a week ago I get this call from Helen saying she wants me to do this job here. Only when I get here, she suddenly calls again and tells me forget it. Go home.

So?

So I ask why. And she says it cuz my mark's already dead. So I do a little checkin' around, and the guy's like totally alive, brah.

So how's that a set-up??

Why would she lie to me, brah? Why would she send me here, then change everything around and pretend the guy's dead?

Jarret can think of a few reasons why.

Wait, there's more!

All I want to know is how you found me.

Rafa gets a funny look as if it's obvious.

You're like a creature of habits, dude.

He indicates Jarret's fruit bowl as evidence.

Same way that gnarly dude found you.

What dude?

The dude that's been following you, brah, or hadn't you noticed?

What's he look like?

'Bout my size. Sunglasses. I didn't exactly like take a picture, all right? Point is if nobody supposedly knows you're here, why's somebody followin' you? And why's Helen lyin' to me? Somethin like major sketchy's goin' down, brah. And if you ask me, it's all fallin' right down on top of us!

Jarret considers stoically. He finally turns to Rafa:

Here's what you're going to do—

Anything, brah—

You're going to go to the airport, and get on the first plane home. You understand?

Rafa's face fills with a disappointed incredulity.

Home? I was thinkin maybe you and me, we could work together. You know, figure this shit out. once and for all.

Go home, Rafa, but don't tell anybody. Understand? Don't talk to anybody.

Rafa's face twists into suspicion.

Thought you were my friend.

Leave here today, Rafa, and no friend will ever give you better advice.

But I could help you!

Goodbye, Rafa.

Jarret moves off, disappearing into the crowded avenue. Out of Rafa's view, he takes out his phone, tempted to confront Helen, but thinks better and tucks it away again.

Arriving at the public square, the familiar 20's man in the yellow headband approaches him again, holding out another leaflet.

Big rally Saturday, mistuh. You come, okay?

Jarret accepts the leaflet, noting the guy's courage, but keeps moving. But the young man keeps pace, wanting to say more.

If Police see tourist, they no do nothing, okay?

Jarret is about to respond, but then moves on and enters the office building. Once inside, he stops to look back at the square to check if he's been followed. Scanning the Bahru supporters, he can't help but note their undaunted faces, their willingness to risk their lives.

Pushing the thought aside, he heads up the stairs, trying to escape back into the predictability of his task, the precision of his work.

Climbing the stairs past the various businesses, he passes unnoticed as he makes his way to the roof.

Moments later he steps out onto it again and, checking the office building behind him, moves to his sniper's nest to check the air duct for his rifle. As he does, finding it safely hidden inside, he hears police sirens whining up from the city's din in the distance, growing louder as they draw closer.

Jarret elbows out to the roof's ledge, where he peers down to see police cars racing up into the square below and screeching to halt to unload another contingent of officers. Spilling out of the police cars, they angle again for the young man with the yellow headband as the Bahru volunteers scatter.

The officers manage to corner the young man this time near the newly constructed podium. They quickly wrestle him to the ground as Sergeant Tre arrives in another car. He orders them to drag their helpless prey around the side of the building, out of the square's view.

Compelled by what he knows is about to happen, Jarret, keeping low, retreats from the ledge and makes his way to the side ledge of the building's roof, where he peeks over to see Tre smirking with satisfaction as his men gang-beat the helpless young man into bloody submission, taking turns with their batons and fists to punish his body even after it droops, unconscious.

Jarret continues to watch, filling with an ancient rage as Tre takes a laughing piss on his victim's broken, bleeding face much to the delight of his men, who offer him a celebratory cigarette, unaware Jarret is looking down at them like an angry god, committing their acts, and their faces, to memory.

As they head back out into the public square, Jarret creeps back over to his sniper's perch to watch them climb back into their cars and drive away, laughing and congratulating each other.

Jarret sits back, reeling and then suddenly rushes back over to check on the young man and sees his comrades quickly returning to carry him way.

Jarret slumps again and looks up, skyward, to see the gray clouds drift silently by as the day retreats into evening.

Pulling himself together, he shoulders the rucksack, taking the rifle with him, now leaving nothing to chance.

As the shadows grow, he steps from the office building and walks back across the now-quiet square, still echoing with the attack–the kind of viciousness that takes its pleasure from inflicting pain, the kind he had long ago numbed himself to, steeled himself against. So why should it so affect him now?

He pauses, stopping to gather himself again before continuing on into the marketplace, making his way back to his hotel, filling with the dread of a reckoning that has finally come to claim its own. It is then that he hears:

Reynolds?

Instantly recognizing Lia's voice, he turns to see her catching up to him, her face full of a tacit knowing and shadows.

Come with me. I want you to see something.

He hesitates, worried that he's shouldering the rucksack holding the rifle.

Please.

He succumbs, following her gentle lead as she guides him back through the avenues to the Wayang stage where another audience has gathered to watch a play, performed alone tonight by the Dalang.

As puppets dance in shadowy silhouettes to the crowd's delight, Jarret eyes Lia, confused as to why she has brought him here. As if answering his wordless question, she takes his hand and finds them a place where they can see the play, leans in close to him and whispers, narrating the action.

An evil Scorpion king is worried a village boy will one day defeat him. So the Scorpion King hires an alligator to kill the boy.

The men, women and children erupt with laughter at something.

So why are they laughing?

Because everyone knows the Scorpion King is General Matak, and the boy, Bahru.

And the alligator?

She allows the raucous play to come to an end without answering, then takes in the audience's loud applause with satisfaction.

Jarret looks at her, still awaiting an answer.

Come.

Minutes later they are windblown, squeezed together into the back of a rickshaw hurrying through the balmy night, escaping the city lights for the wealthy suburbs.

Lia gives directions to their driver in Bahasa then leans back, into the world of her private, sojourning thoughts. Jarret notes her withdrawal, feeling the hypnotic rush of humid air playing in her hair. He looks away, trying to disengage, to halt her effect on him only to be drawn back by the warm, unconscious rub and bump of her shoulder against his as the rickshaw huuries on over the uneven roads.

Lulled by its roll and bounce, he finds himself drifting, dreaming, until Lia touches his hand and he looks up to find her indicating a heavily guarded compound, its entrance fortified by sandbag berms and armed soldiers, defending a long driveway leading to an estate home.

Jarret notes it and then looks back to Lia for an explanation.

General Matak's compound.

Jarret absorbs that and then remembers he shouldn't know who that is.

Who's that?

Our next president, if he gets his way. And he could, because the police will help him.

Why?

She shrugs, as if reciting the oldest news in the world.

Money. He pays them off.

And where does he get the money?

He steals it. International aid meant for the poor. Drugs. You name it. It pays to be a General.

She says something to the driver in Bahasa and he swings the rickshaw around to head back the way they came. As they pass by Matak's estate again, Jarret takes a last look and then turns to Lia.

That's what you wanted to show me?

You healed him, you know.

Who?

The boy. From the other night.

Jarret sobers.

No. I didn't.

She eyes him implying that it was a certainty. So he turns to look out at the blur of lights washing past them, dismissing even the possibility.

You did.

Lia then seems to let it go and looks out her window. Finally:

I see what you see. Auras. Just as I see yours. So does my father.

She turns to him again, her knowing gaze disarming him, undoing him, offering, it seems, to free him, yet also somehow beckoning forth the darkness in him, the buried secrets on which everything in him has forever been precariously, delicately poised.

He turns away from her, afraid, and they travel on in silence.

Back in Dalang and Lia's garden, a star-filled sky arcs slowly overhead, silently creeping toward dawn. He takes a sip of tea and looks up to find them gazing at him deeply, peering at him as if they can see his soul.

He instantly recoils, wanting to retreat back into the safety of the shadows of his isolated world yet feeling as if he no longer can.

Dalang takes a long puff off a clove cigarette and tilts his head.

So, how it feel to you when happening?

Jarret hesitates, deciding whether to engage.

He means when the healing energy flows through you.

Jarret's first instinct is deny, but then realizes he can't.

...Like it has a life of its own.

Dalang puts down his tea, nodding.

And do you have life of your own?

I have to go.

Dalang says something in Bahasa, which Lia seems to doubt the wisdom of translating. But Dalang insists.

The spinning wheels on their brow, throat, torsos are Chakras.

Jarret eyes her. Waits for more.

The life centers where the body, soul and spirit meet.

And you know this because?

Because we see them, too.

Jarret thinks about it, panicking, and gets up.

I need to go.

Soon, he's fleeing warily back through the busy marketplace, alive with the evening's crowd. But his only interest is getting back to the sanctuary of his hotel room and his purpose, his job, the thing he understands and controls. As he moves on, starting to coax back again the proper perspective for a man in his profession, he hears:

It's him! That's the man!

A tiny, excited woman points over at him as he passes. So he quickens his pace, moving to escape her attention. But she pursues him, determined, calling after him, alerting others ahead of him.

He heal my son! With his hands!

With no other choice, he turns to confront her, instantly recognizing her as the round-faced, young mother of the boy. But he pretends they've never met.

Can I help you, ma'am?

You heal my son!

Others around them take notice:

You must be confusing me with somebody else.

As Jarret tries to extricate himself, she pursues him with certainty:

No. Is you! You save my boy!

Jarret tries to maneuver away, but she won't let him go:

He save my son with his hands!

She catches up to him again and tries to kiss his hand, but Jarret recoils as even more gather around them.

I show you. I show you.

She calls into the marketplace.

Petit! Where are you? Come!!

Her son–the boy Jarret laid hands on–steps into view, now looking healthy. Restored. Jarret sobers, trying to hide his shock.

You see? You heal him! You heal him! He well, all because you!

No, you're...mistaken.

Jarret moves off again, darting away into the city traffic, dodging across lanes of oncoming cars, buses and motor scooters that honk and swerve, barely missing him as he hurries away.

Back in his room, he paces, no longer able to sit. His phone rings. Steeling himself, he picks up.

That you, Tiger?

What is it?

It's about your meet.

He storms over, anticipating what comes next.

What about it?

It's been, well, delayed. But only a little.

How little?

Just twenty-four little hours.

He looks around, his mind already seizing on this opportunity.

But it's for-sure Sunday now.

I told you, Helen, any more delays and I'd be done.

I know ya did, sugar, but ya gotta believe me when I say there wasn't anythin' I could do. Somethin' about a family illness. But all we're talkin' is twenty-four more little hours, baby. That's all. And then it's done. And I won't ever ask ya for anythin' ever again.

That's not the point.

No, the point is we both could retire on what you're set ta make.

Who else knows I'm here, Helen?

What are ya talkin' 'bout?

Who else?
Nobody! Why on earth would ya think that?
He clicks off, considerrs, then starts quickly gathering up his things.

An airport terminal.
Rows of back-to-back seating.
Jarret tensely awaiting his flight.

As travelers and tourists hurry past him, he looks up at the flight board and checks his watch, relying on the thought that this will all be over soon.

But as the final minutes to his flight tick past, he starts to gaze around at his fellow travelers, observing the dim glow of their auras as they move about, oblivious, making their phone calls, marching to their schedules, running from their moment as surely as he has been running from his.

Stunned by the sudden revelation, he sits down again, momentarily unable to breathe as one discovery draws in another. All his efforts, all his planning, all his preparations, practice, endless isolation, focus, efforts, the years spent escaping or hiding, all of it was only an effort to delay, escape the inevitable truth, the certain end. Just like all these people. Just like the world. Except that somewhere deep inside him, somewhere under the opaque layers of the mud and loam of his past, beneath all the reasons and rationales buried in his being, there is another truth, a different truth, a truth now burning up before his mind like a dark diamond, revealing glimpses the desperate, broken and beaten boy at his core–the terrified boy who believed he could somehow prevent his own moment by offering another's in its place.

As the discovery lingers as if suspended in the ether before him, reflecting him, revealing him, releasing him from its secret pact, he hears:
We have ta stop meetin like this, sugar.
He is startled when he feels the force of Helen's unmistakable voice drop on him like an anvil.
Folks will talk.
He turns his head, the colors quickly fading as he discovers Helen, seated on the same cushioned bench but facing the opposite direction, maintaining the appearance of strangers for the benefit of the airport's omnipresent security cameras.
Flight 371 to Los Angeles now boarding at Gate 2.
Without looking at each other, they speak.

Sorry I can't stay and chat, Helen, but I'd miss my flight.

Ya don't know how sorry I am ta hear that. And after comin all this way, too.

Jarret eyes the quickly-forming line at his boarding gate, realizing he still has a few minutes more before he must go.

Why'd you have me followed?

Fella doesn't answer his phone, what's a girl ta do?

Find another fella.

She smirks, bemused.

Story of my life, lover.

Thought Rafa was your fella.

Rafa? That little piece of dung? Only reason I had him here was so he could be your fall guy. Or hadn't ya figured that out yet?

He hadn't.

Told ya I made all the arrangements, didn't I? Which has always included lookin' after you.

Thought it was you who needed looking after.

Still do. But here ya are, skippin' town on me. Doesn't exactly make ya my knight-in-shinin'-armor, now does it?

He shoulders the rucksack, determined to go.

Guess ya musta spent all your chivalry on that little, yellow local tramp.

Caught off guard, his eyes storm.

Oops. Did I strike a nerve, baby?

Just how long have you been here, Helen?

Long enough, lover-boy. Long enough.

Flight 371 to Los Angeles, now boarding at Gate 2.

Jarret glances over at his gate—it's time to go.

That makes two of us. Good-by, Helen.

Nothin' I can say to make ya stay?

I did what I said I'd do. And then some.

Oh come on now, ya really gonna make me have ta point out the obvious?

Jarret eyes the gate, needing to go, but turns one last time:

Meaning what?

Meanin' either ya stay, and do what you do best, or who knows what might happen ta that two-bit skank whore, and her puppet-happy pappy.

Jarret's body tightens. His eyes burn.

Which is ta say, somethin bad definitely will most likely happen, handsome, if ya go.

Last call for flight 371 to Los Angeles, boarding at Gate 2.

You're making a mistake, Helen.

Actually, I'm just takin" out a little insurance, which I shouldn't have ta, darlin. But knowin" ya as I do, I figured I best come prepared.

If you do anything, to either one of them.

Long as ya do what I need done, they gonna be just fine. Just fine.

Jarret watches an airline attendant close the boarding gate, clearing the flight to depart. Helen shrugs as if this was all inevitable:

Anyway, I'll let ya get back ta work. Oh, by the way, Sunday's a go. 10am sharp. And don't worry. It'll all be over soon. See ya later, Alligator.

As she moves off into the terminal, he watches after, stung but quickly galvanizing into a new plan.

He steps from the terminal into the humid, exhaust-scented breeze and strides back over to the driver who just rickshaw'd him over here, much to the driver's surprise.

As the afternoon gives way to evening, Jarret moves about the city, checking with various bartenders, prostitutes, street-corner hustlers and street urchins asking after Rafa, describing him, his earrings, all to no avail.

As the evening's shadows grow, he heads back into the marketplace, angling for Daksa's booth, hungry and tired. But as he draws near, he pulls up short, stunned to see Rafa casually chomping down a bowl of fruit while chatting with Daksa.

Jarret slows, incredulous, then moves forward cautiously, certain that Rafa has planned this little rendezvous.

Rafa, sensing Jarret's arrival, just keeps munching and chatting as if he wasn't there.

We need to talk, Rafa.

Do we?

Turns out you were right.

Rafa nods as if taking this all in, only to suddenly turn and jab his finger into Jarret's chest.

Goddamn right I was right! And as for your great idea about me leavin here? Wrong again, dude, cause that's exactly what you-know-who was waitin for me to do!

Helen?

Goddamn right, Helen.

Rafa starts munching on his fruit again, only to suddenly spit it out, alarming Daksa, who looks to Jarret, confused. But Jarret remains implacable, allowing Rafa his rant.

Goddamn bitch. And you? You're her bitch!

Not only is it a set-up, Rafa, but you're the fall guy.

No shit. Only question I got is why tell me? Huh? Why not just let me fall?

Because I thought you might want do something about it.

Like what?

Like find a way out of this.

Rafa sobers and looks up at Jarret as if he might be ready to consider a proposal.

Ya mean like work together?

Yes. But since I just wasted a whole afternoon trying to find you, so if you're in, we need to get to work now.

Rafa eyes him, seeming to weigh the possibilities. Then asks:

And how do I know this isn't just part of the set-up, too, brah? The part where you, havin' failed to convince me to leave, now ya try to convince me to stay just so you and Helen can make sure I never leave.

How do you know, Rafa? You don't. But given what you do know, I'd say under the circumstances, I'm your last and best bet.

Would you? Which would also have to mean that you need me. You want my help, is that it? Suddenly I'm not the problem child who doesn't know shit anymore, am I?

As Jarret eyes him, he starts to see dim, boiling hues radiating faintly to life around Rafa's head.

Yes or no, Rafa?

Tell you what: I'm going to do for you exactly what you did for me when I needed your help.

Rafa shunts up his middle finger in Jarret's face, then spins on his heel and heads off into the marketplace.

As Jarret watches after him, he hears:

Why he waste food?

Jarret turns to see the incredulous look on Daksa's face. He then looks back after Rafa. But as Jarret turns to go, he feels another rush of energy storm through him, indicating the onset of another attack.

And a moment later, he's knocking on Lia and Dalang's door. Lia opens it as if expecting him and moves off, leaving the door open for

Jarret to enter. So he does, and finds them waiting for what he's come to say.

You both need to leave here. Now.

Lia looks calmly over to Dalang, then back at Jarret, unmoved.

They will kill you if you stay here.

Dalang shrugs as if he is unconcerned.

They kill you, too.

Maybe. But you can hide.

Lia shakes her head, dismissing any such effort.

Where? There will be no place to hide. Not under Matak.

You could at least try?

Dalang shrugs.

And what will you be doing while we try?

Their eyes now bore into him, confronting him. But instead of guilt, he feels anger boiling up inside him:

So you won't even try?

Lia shakes her, unyielding.

Then I guess I tried.

They do not respond, so Jarret starts out only to hear Dalang call after him.

They come for you, Reynolds. They come to kill you, too. And you can no hide. No from them. No from you.

Jarret slows, turns, boiling over with a sudden rage that wants words, but can find none.

But Lia holds her ground, matching his intensity with her own. He turns to leave again, only to feel a bolt of energy surge through him, causing his body to spasm. He drops to his knees to keep from falling outright as another jolt of electricity cripples him, dropping him to all fours.

Goddamnit!

Another bolt shocks through him, disabling even his attempts to resist.

But Dalang and Lia do not move to assist him. Instead, they wait, not lending him a hand, leaving him to this moment which is his alone.

Frog in well think he safe. But no safe. Find no peace.

Jarret tries to stand, only to be rocked by another incapacitating spasm which sends him right back down to the ground. As he rides out its wave he hears:

Want get out of well?

Jarret, slowly gathering himself, looks up at Dalang desperately. Dalang asks again:

Yes, or no?

Still carrying the rucksack with him, packed with its lethal secret, Jarret and Lia follow Dalang back down the dark, winding dirt roads of the slums, past rows of corrugated metal dwellings to the hut with the hung-canvas door.

Entering, they find an abode full of sick men, women and children, awaiting their arrival like pilgrims.

Jarret is shocked, halted by the sight of them and looks to Dalang who beckons him onwards. But he's unable to move, daunted by the human devastation all around him. Their bloodshot eyes are all looking up to him, entreating him, placing all their hopes on him.

Lia finally pinches his arm and he moves on to find a small table as before, set up in the back.

I can't do this.

Lia throws a faded bed sheet over the table.

Then who will?

He wants to run, escape, but Lia's steady gaze stops him.

If running away from yourself had worked, you wouldn't be here.

Over the next hours, Lia and Dalang escort the sick and suffering to Jarret's table, where he cups his hands under their heads, or over their wounds, sometimes feeling something surge through him, at other times not, but always seeing the eager, worried or grateful faces looking up at him as if he was the face of the divine.

One after the other step or limp forward, a procession of maladies spurned by the world, perpetuated by their poverty, the squalor and abject neglect of every day, leaving them to the casual derision, revulsion and hatred that have always attended the poor—their diseases, disabilities and deformities seeming more and more to Jarret like a procession of Wayang puppet characters, embodying the death dance, the ruin of the world.

He administers to all, feeling more like an observer than a participant.

Between each two patients, Lia pours water over his hands and then hands him a towel to dry, cooling and cleansing him.

It helps to clear the energy, from one to the next.

Jarret has no idea what she means, but obeys, so far from anything he understands that he begins to feel like a child.

When he finishes, Lia nods he's done and, collecting his rucksack, he emerges from the back room to see most are still there waiting for him. As he walks between them, confused, they smile and nod, thanking him in the only way they can, drawing him back to something deep inside him, like a memory too painful to reveal, a wound too deep to heal.

He then walks home with Lia and Dalang in silence.

Later that night, back at Lia and Dalang's home, he finds himself once again sitting in their back room where Dalang keeps the chest filled with his puppets. As he eyes it, all goes dark. And as he struggles to see again, he wakes to find himself on the office building's roof, looking down at the public square, deserted and empty in the twilight.

He then hears the rhythmic rattle of drums and cymbals announcing a procession, so he edges forward and peeks over the roof's ledge to see a march of Wayang puppets, large as men, dancing in their slow, weightless way, their every elongated gesture a revelation of character, every grotesque feature embodying, distilling the parade of human archetypes.

As they circle the square, they suddenly slow, their drumming stops and they all look up slowly to Jarret.

He quickly hides away, jerking back from the ledge. Only silence follows. But then he begins to hear a crowd chanting "Bahru, Bahru, Bahru."

A moment later, his eyes shunt open to find himself back in the puppets' room, but with the chant still echoing in the morning air. He bolts up, dizzy, trying to get his bearings and grabs his rucksack.

He moves off into their home, searching for Lia and Dalang, calling their names, only to realize they're gone. He instantly deduces where they must have gone.

Out in the marketplace, he follows the echoing chants back to the public square to find it filled with supporters, chanting, waving Bahru placards alongside hand-made posters bearing the likeness of their fallen comrade, the young, yellow-headband man.

Sensing doom, Jarret pushes his way into the crowd, asking:
What day is it?
Someone offers back Saturday as he spots Lia and Dalang and moves to pluck them from the crowd. But they resist, wanting to

participate in the rally for as long as they can when they suddenly hear the whine of approaching Police sirens, igniting an instant panic.

As all move to escape the square, a flood of baton-wielding police sweep into the marketplace, surrounding the rally, beating and arresting as many Bahru supporters as they can. The melee soon spills into the marketplace and into the city's streets, creating havoc and panic like a wild fire spreading across a city.

Jarret pulls Lia and Dalang through the frenzied confusion to a side avenue, leading them away as fast as he can to an alley where he hails a rickshaw and helps Dalang climb in. Then he turns to Lia.

Get in!

No.

You need to go, Lia.

They need my help.

Goddamnit, would you just get the hell out of here!

No.

Seeing it's no use to argue with her, he yells to the Rickshaw driver:

Get him out of here!

Lia says something to her father in Bahasa, then watches as the Rickshaw speeds away.

As baton-wielding police rush into the city streets, Jarret pushes Lia behind him, waits for one the officers to swing his baton and, slipping just beyond its range, grabs it on its downward arc, twisting it from the officer's hand while sweep-kicking the second officer's legs out from under him.

Hitting the first with his own baton, he then steals the gun away from the second, offering the first officer a chance to flee, which he does. He then grabs Lia and rushes her away, ready to defend her against any comers as they search for a path out of the panic gripping the city.

But the riot is spreading like a gasoline fire, with more people and police pouring out everywhere, causing bottlenecks and stampedes as terrorized marchers, rioters, shoppers and merchants rush about, hell-bent on escaping the coming crush of thrashing batons.

Jarret beats back a frenzied mob, pulling Lia to safety just as she was about to be trampled under by their mindless crush. He then leads her through a back-alley to an adjoining street where passersby are only now becoming aware of growing disturbance, alarmed by the sudden crack of tear gas guns.

As confusion grips the city, Jarret and Lia slip away, keeping their heads low as they angle back to Jarret's seedy hotel, dodging white wafts of burning tear gas clouds.

Entering his room, they lock the door and stop to catch their breaths, their eyes burning from the gas as they ride out the adrenaline rush still coursing through their veins.

He pours her a glass of water. She drinks it down, succumbing to a raft of emotions, which all come to rest on him. He waits, confused.

What?

Thank you

He eyes her, lost. Still confused.

For what?

Lia moves to him and wraps her arms around him. He allows it, slow at first to hold her back, but then succumbing, releasing his arms to hold her, to feel the heat of her body pressing into his, to feel her racing heart, her breathing, her need urging his, conjuring him back from the depths, the darkness, drawing the splintered shadows of his psyche back into itself, back into himself, raw, untouched until now. A moment later they are on the room's untouched bed, clamoring for each, gripping, clutching, melding as the Police sirens wail, the crowds panic, and the crack of rifle-fire last deep into the night.

In the hours before dawn, as Lia showers, he finds himself lying on the bed as the distant, sporadic sounds of rioting continues somewhere in the distance. He gets up and flips on the TV to look for news, but finds again only footage of General Matak greeting his friendly crowds, beseeching him as if he were a god.

As her shower hisses in the background, he watches the newsreel unwind, watching the relentless parade of graft and betrayal, replete with the requisite caricatures who deem themselves better than the rest. Then his phone rings, shocking him back to the moment. He quickly checks the number and clicks on.

Hey.

He braces himself.

What?

Heard there was some trouble. Just makin sure you're okay.

Who am I working for, Helen?

Excuse me?

I want to know who the client is.

Ours is not to reason why, babe?
Who is it, Helen?
Ask me if they pay. Then ask me if it matters.
I want to know.
No ya don't, sugar. That's why ya always let me do the talkin for ya all these years—exactly cuz ya don't wanna know.

Lia steps out from the bathroom, wrapped in a towel.

Jarret clicks off the call, wanting desperately to make this secret moment between them last just a little longer.

I think it would be best if I didn't go home tonight.
Stay here.

As she moves to climb into bed, he gets up, and moves to sit in the chair. She waits in the bed, confused.

If you can't sleep, I won't sleep either.
No, I...sleep this way.
In a chair?
I'm used to it.
But...why?
Just always have.

She waits, sensing more.

Since when?
Since...

She still waits.

...one of my mother's boyfriends poured gasoline on my bed, and lit it.

She looks at him, horrified.

I wasn't in it. But I'd stuffed my pillow to make it look like I was. I was hiding in the closet, And as he stood there, waiting for me to scream, that's when I...
What?
Hit him from behind with a hammer.

Lia holds him with her eyes as the moment hangs in the air.

Feeling as if gravity has let go of him, he seems to be weightless for a moment, no longer tied to the earth. But then he hears her voice, as if calling him back:

Come. Lie beside me.

He hesitates, wary, perplexed. But the look in her eyes compels him, and he finally gets up from the chair, and lies down beside her. And she wraps herself around him, protecting him with her body, her life-force. Something he had never felt before. And he falls asleep.

In his dream, he finds himself looking through his rifle-scope, peering down through its magnifying lens at Bahru as he steps up to the podium, surrounded by throngs of supporters, bunting and banners.

He adjusts the scope's cross-hairs so that they meet on Bahru's exposed forehead, framing the kill shot as Bahru waves to the crowd. As Jarret's index finger slides over the trigger, Bahru launches into an earnest speech. Jarret begins to squeeze down on the lever, his finger tightening on the trigger, about to reach its tipping point when he hears someone chuckling—not at Bahru—but somehow at him.

He pulls back from his scope to look over the square, searching the crowd for the source of the mocking laugh but cannot find it.

So he looks back through his scope, panning quickly over Bahru's supporters until he finds an empty spot and everything goes silent, except for the laughter.

Panning quickly back into where the crowd just stood, he now finds an empty, deserted public square. All have vanished. So he sweeps his scope back and forth over the square to finally discover Helen and Rafa, standing out in the open, embracing like rapid lovers as Rafa devours her neck and breasts while Helen, grinning, gazes up at Jarret, mocking him, baiting him.

A knock in the night wakes Jarret with a start. He sits up, alarmed as another knock shocks Lia awake, and she sits up, too.

He motions for her to hide, so she slides down from bed and closes herself inside the closet as he gets up, stepping lightly, readying the gun he took from the officer, and positions himself behind the door.

Hello? Is Daksa. Everything-fresh-today, Daksa?

Jarret shoots a look to Lia, who doesn't know what to do.

Dalang need to see you, okay?

Jarret cracks open the door.

You come alone?

Yes. Someone try to follow, but I too fast.

Jarret looks past Daksa, checking the hallway.

How'd you find us?

I ask around.

Daksa shrugs, apologizing it was so easy.

Okay. Give us a minute.

Jarret beckons to Lia, who starts pulling on her clothes as Daksa shakes his head.

No. Just you.
Why just me?
That what he say. I think he afraid she in too much danger.
That's what convinces Jarret. He looks back to Lia.
I'll go. You wait here.

Daksa leads Jarret on a back-alley way through the city, using his street-savvy knowledge of its byways to avoid detection.

Soon they are passing again through the shanty-towns, moving through their squalid streets in the harsh, stark light of day to arrive once more at the corrugated metal dwelling from a night ago.

Entering, Daksa leads him back to the room improvised for his use where Dalang is waiting for him.

So. How is frog?

Dalang smiles. Jarret eases. Shrugs.

Dalang then gets up, steps out for a moment, and returns escorting a sick teenage boy with his apprehensive mother.

This Jiwa, and Jiwa mother, Ani.

Jarret looks to Dalang, confused.

Just one this time?

Her full name is Ani Bahru. She Bahru wife. This boy his son.

Jarret sobers, his compartmentalized worlds colliding.

He then senses another's presence entering the small room and turns to see Bahru, stepping humbly forward to comfort his wife and son. Jarret, not knowing what else to do, focuses on Jiwa, cupping his hands around the sick boy's head as the room grows silent.

But there are no colors, no twitching or trembling of energy; just the silence of the moment filling the room like a prayer.

Afterwards, Bahru steps forward extending his hand.

Thank you.

As they shake hands he says:

Your hands are very warm.

One of Bahru's Aides rushes in to whisper something in Bahru's ear. A look of concern fills Bahru's face and he turns to his wife.

It would be safer if we left separately.

His wife nods. Bahru kisses her, nods to Jarret and then leaves with his aide. Bahru's wife nods to Jarret, grateful, and leaves by another way.

Later, as Jarret steps back out, he finds Dalang waiting for him, smoking a pungent clove cigarette. He eyes Jarret with a knowing directness, comnpelling Jarret to finally ask:

How did you know about me? Who I am? What I am?

One day, assassin in you will kill assassin in you. Because that what assassin do. Yes?

Dalang snuffs out the cigarette.

But how did you know?

Because your colors. They no can lie. So what real name?

Jarret considers, sensing the onset of the rising storm inside him.

Jarret.

Promise me you keep Lia safe, Jarret?

Jarret eyes Dalang, feeling the volumes of upspoken words between them distilling, clarifying into this moment.

I promise.

Daksa steps out. Dalang turns to him.

Take him back.

Jarret nods to Dalang, and follows Daksa who eyes Jarret with a knowing premonition.

You are going to leave soon. Aren't you?

Jarret steps back into his hotel room to find the bed made, but Lia's gone.

Damnit!

He hides the rucksack behind an attic-access panel, and rushes back out.

His heart pounding in his chest, Jarret moves quickly through the crowded marketplace avenues in the afternoon light, angling for Lia's home.

But when he arrives he sees a police car outside with two officers waiting beside it.

Knowing he can't wait, he strides to the front door as if he has every right to enter. But the officers quickly move to block his progress, barking at him in Bahasa and training their weapons.

Sergeant Tre, alerted by their voices, steps out to instantly recognize Jarret.

Mr. Reynolds. What did I tell you about coming here?

Something about how you weren't a puppet, as I recall.

Tre smirks at Jarret's insult, bemused.

Americans always think they know better. That they can do anything they want.

Really? Cause far as I can see, that's how you behave. Or is it that you just want to feel like an American?

Tre manages to maintain his cool.

Come. Maybe you can convince them to cooperate.

Tre leads him into the courtyard where another officer is standing guard over Dalang and Lia, who are bound, gagged, beaten and bleeding.

Jarret controls himself. Bides his time.

I try to get them to tell me what I wanted to know nicely, but they are just so stubborn.

Tre draws a gentle, menacing finger over Lia's swollen cheek for Jarret's benefit. Then smirks up as Jarret's eyes bore into him.

You like tying up women and old men, is that it, Sergeant?

Actually, what I like is...

Tre slaps Lia hard, drawing more blood and then eyes Jarret again, bull-baiting him, wanting him to make his move.

But Jarret remains stoic, depriving him of a reaction, triggering Tre to try even harder. So he punches her.

All Jarret can do is to keep from rushing at him, which Tre's officer is only too ready for.

Real tough guy, huh?

Tre smirks, steps back and lights up a cigarette, takes a few deep drags and then steps forward to snuff it out on Jarret's brow, searing him a third-eye-like welt.

Jarret's jaw clamps as he endures the excruciating burn, but he holds his gaze steady on Tre, unyielding.

So now you're going to tell me who you really are, Mr. Reynolds, and why you are really here.

You really want to know?

As the officers outside finish off their smokes, they hear movement inside the dwelling and look up.

A few beats later, Jarret leans casually out the front door. The instant the other officers see him, they ready their guns.

Your Sergeant wants one of you guys to come in here.

The two officers exchange a look, and the first volunteers.

Keeping his weapon trained on Jarret, he enters, giving Jarret a wide berth.

A moment later, Jarret leans back out of the door again.

Make that both of you.

The second officer hesitates, suspicious. Jarret shrugs.

Whatever. He's your boss, not mine.

Jarret goes back inside.

The officer, left to worry what Tre might do, reconsiders and enters the home cautiously.

He edges in to find everything's quiet. No sign of anybody.

So he grips his gun tighter and steps forward to view the courtyard to see the chairs where Lia and Dalang were being held are now empty, but beside them, on the ground, Tre and the other two officers are lying face down.

As the officer pivots to rush for help, he turns to see Jarret. But as he raises his gun to fire, something slams into the back of his head. His eyes roll and he collapses, leaving Lia standing behind him holding the other fallen officer's rifle like a baseball bat.

Jarret leans out of the door once more to check if the coast's clear and sees several neighbors looking on.

He sobers, not knowing how they'll react. But they give him knowing, reassuring nods, so he proceeds, beckoning for Lia and Dalang, who hurry out and climb into the back of the police car while their neighbors quickly move to clean up the scene.

Jarret climbs into the driver's seat, dons an officer's cap left on the seat, and speeds them away.

As they move back out onto the city streets, garnering incredulous stares from pedestrians and drivers reacting to the pale-faced officer behind the wheel, Jarret decides to flip on the siren.

Accelerating away, he races past several traffic snafus and turns onto the dirt roads along the spillway, where he suddenly brakes hard.

Wait for me at the healing house, all right?

Lia senses doom as they climb out.

Where are you going?

I just need you to wait here for me, all right?

She looks at him deeply, her eyes filling with dread. But he averts his gaze and accelerates away, just as the sound of another police siren wails up over the slums.

As he tries to navigate back out of the slums, losing his way several times down dead ends, he sees a police car racing up from behind in hot pursuit. As he tries to accelerate away, he can see via his rearview mirror that the police officer is radioing for backup.

So Jarret swerves, weaving through the ramshackle roads, chased by a determined vehicle that he can't seem to shake, with more, no doubt, on the way.

He makes another sharp turn down yet another street and then hairpins into a back alley, smashing through a corrugated metal barrier to suddenly find himself airborne…as his police car dives into a spillway, crashing into its stinking muck.

Before he can extricate himself, the Police car chasing him tries to brake in time, but can't, and its momentum carries it out over the spillway…to crash nose-first into the trunk of Jarret's vehicle—but without the mud to cushion its impact—causing its officer-diver to slam his head into the steering wheel, knocking him out.

Jarret, shaken, pushes open his vehicle's door into the muck and climbs out, sinking in the sewage as he fords his way back to the spillway's banks.

Back on the dirt road above the sewage, he pulls out his phone on the move and calls Helen. A few rings and Helen picks up.

Where are you?

New deal.

What're ya talkin 'bout?

You want me to take the meeting tomorrow morning, you're going to take them back with you.

Take who back where?

Guess.

Oh for Christ'ssake, honey, there's some things even I can't do!

Then deal's off, and the meeting's off, too.

Jarret waits to hear what she'll do.

Ever hear of a little somethin' called customs?

Now what's customs to a woman like you?

A long pause hangs in the air. Finally:

One. I can do one.

Both.

One. You decide which, and have them meet me outside the Rose Hotel in at nine-thirty sharp. But just so we're clear: if I do this, and you don't take care of my business, I ain't takin' any prisoners.

Neither will I, Helen.

Then I guess we understand each other, darlin'.

He clicks off, taking a moment to fathom what he's done, then looks around, trying to get his bearings to see locals coming out of their doors to check him out, curious, suspicious.

One recognizes him--an old woman from a night ago. She smiles and raises her hand, greeting him.

Where's the house? Take me to the house?

She points, indicating she knows what he's asking, and leads him where he needs to go.

Jarret enters to find them waiting for him, Lia looking worried, Dalang meditating but he opens his eyes to gaze up knowingly at him.

I can keep her safe, but she would have to leave here.

Lia looks up, shocked.

What are you talking about?

Lia looks at her father, incredulous.

Go with him.

Go with him where?

She turns back to Jarret.

An associate of mine's going to take you back to America.

America? I'm not going anywhere without my father.

Jarret looks to Dalang. Dalang looks to Lia.

You must go.

No. Not without you.

Please do as he say.

I can't. I won't!

Dalang says something in Bahasa. Lia's eyes begin to well with tears as he turns back to Jarret.

You keep her safe. Yes?

Lia rushes into her father's arms, as Jarret looks on, reeling.

Dalang hugs Lia, knowing it could be the last time and then eases her back from him, eyeing her firmly, gently.

Moving again, making their way through the riot-ravaged streets, Jarret lays out the plan: Lia's to meet Helen. He then gives her the address of a safe hotel in Los Angels, and the location of his storage unit, and where he hides its key.

I will do this, for my father, but only if you keep him safe.

I'll do everything I can.

She eyes him, not knowing if this is goodbye.

You have someplace to stay tonight?

She nods, looking as if she would otherwise kiss him, then disappears into the streets. He now doubles back to his room, retrieves the rucksack, and heads back out.

As he steps back out, Daksa, waiting across the street, calls to him and runs over.

I know a place you can stay.

Jarret, grateful, nods, and Daksa leads him away, taking Jarret to his home which turns out to be a lean-to under a bridge.

You'll be safe here.

As Daksa starts to leave.

Where are you going?

To get you some fruit.

Daksa smiles and disappears, leaving Jarret to watch the skies grow dark from under a bridge.

As he looks up through its wooden planks, seeing only slits of the sky, he feels like a frog, looking up through the darkness, wondering what's above him and, in the absence of truth, supplying his own.

He then notices a salvaged piece of broken mirror, and slowly raises its asymmetrical shape to view himself, seeing now not auras or chakras, but himself, unadorned, looking to himself in this jagged cut of uneven glass like a caricature, a marionette, playing his part in a grotesque play.

Lowering the mirror, he looks back up at the night, feeling as if his whole life has been lived at the bottom of a deep, deep well.

But then Daksa returns, smiling, bringing him a bowl of fruit, pressing it at him, and Jarret suddenly feels as if he can't accept it.

Daksa insists, nodding, so Jarret finally allows it, and Daksa moves off again into the night, undaunted by his circumstances, determined, alive with a freedom that Jarret, for all his independence, has never known.

The long night scrapes by, demanding its requisite wages of restlessness and worry.

In the cool morning air, Jarret's shaken from his thoughts by the distant beat of a djembe drum and the rising chants of "Bahru, Bahru, Bahru" echoing up from the city's heart.

Shaking off the night, he checks his watch: 9:05 a.m.

Gathering himself quickly, shouldering his rucksack, he sets out, resigned to doing what he must to guarantee Lia's safety.

Making his way back to the marketplace, he finds groups of marchers waving Bahru banners, chanting, banging drums, and joining up with other Bahru supporters in a procession to the public square.

He follows them, blending in, using them for cover, only to soon find that something's causing a bottleneck up ahead.

Jarret moves from the supporters to discover its cause, and sees Tre's officers are body searching every person trying to enter the square.

So he reverses pivot, realizing he's going to have to improvise a way back into the office building and back to his sniper's perch.

He finds an alley that cuts along the back of the office building and, climbing up a pile of boxes, hoists himself up into a second-story window. Then, checking if the coast's clear, he breaks its glass, un-locks it and pushes it open to shimmy his way inside, cutting his hand on a shard. As a steady stream of blood begins to flow from his palm, he hustles up the stairwell, angling for the roof, shouldering the rucksack.

Stepping out onto the roof, he can hear the loud, echoing din of the growing crowd below.

Checking the building behind him for any onlookers, he creeps back to his sniper's perch, and unzips the rucksack to retrieve the rifle case.

As he quickly assembles it, loading several cartridges into its magazine, he begins to hear a new, spontaneous round of Bahru, Bahru, Bahru thundering up from the square. So he edges forward and peeks over the roof's ledge. He sees that not only has the crowd swollen, but so has the police presence, lining the square in riot gear as if hoping for a provocation, even if they have to manufacture it themselves.

As the morning's sun rises behind him, he peers through his rifle-sight to see the podium, telescoped, just as a new, loud commotion heralds Bahru's arrival.

Jarret pans his scope to view Bahru, surrounded by aides, climbing from a van as his adoring public crushes in.

Welcome. Welcome all! calls an aide's voice from the podium, readying to introduce Bahru to the crowd.

A deafening cheer thunders up from the square.

Thank you all for coming.

The Aide then restates the welcome in Bahasa and continues on to introduce Bahru's wife, who steps forward to smile and wave and then

Bahru's son, who steps to the podium to smile and wave, looking the picture of health.

Jarret stares at him, astonished, proof of the healing in his hands which are now gripping a rifle, poised to take a life.

The thought rattles him, and he loses his grip. But thinking again of Lia, he reasserts his hold on the rifle, having made his deal.

As Helen waits, checking her watch, Lia looks on from up the block, seeing Helen's true colors.

Helen finally gives up, and goes back into the hotel.

Back in the square, another loud cheer soars up from the crowd as the aide introduces Bahru.

Jarret, watching Bahru through his scope, lines up his target in his crosshairs, trying to rediscover the clarity he once knew at such moments.

But a wash of unfamiliar emotions instead are welling up inside him, connecting him to this moment instead of separating him from it, making Bahru the subject to what he is about to do, not the object.

As Bahru steps to the podium to gracefully accept his supporters' adulation, signaling he's ready to speak, the crowd shouts their approval all the more, releasing, it seems, a lifetime of pent-up hopes and dreams, long suppressed, but now seeming so close to being possible…

Only after this sustained reception do Bahru's good-humored pleas finally quiet the crowd so that he can speak, and the square finally settles down.

As Jarret continues to hold him clearly in his sights, the opportunity is ripe and waiting, but Jarret is struggling, fighting with himself to squeeze the trigger.

Brothers, sisters, how far we have come, and how far we must still go to secure the freedoms for which so many of us have fought and died.

As another explosion of applause roars up from the crowd, Jarret redoubles his effort, his jaw clenching, his body tightening as he wills himself to shoot, to pull the trigger, to save Lia.

But as he eyes Bahru through the telescoping lens, so close to him that it feels as if he is standing in front of him, Jarret begins to see Bahru's aura, glowing up with gold and yellow hues, tinged with turquoise.

Shaken, his momentum interrupted, Jarret is forced once more to look away, gather himself, and then look back through his scope and line up his shot.

As he does, Bahru turns to the police lining the square in riot gear and addresses them in Bahasa, making a special overture of peace on behalf of the people.

But the officers, under orders, only glare back threateningly from behind their shields. One pulls off his helmet, drawing Jarret's attention. And he notices Tre, his face cut and bruised by Jarret's fists, sneering back at Bahru, smug, relishing the violence he's about to unleash.

Jarret, realizing his window of opportunity is fast closing, pans his scope back to Bahru to line up the kill shot once more. As he positions his crosshairs again on Bahru's brow, pressing his index finger slowly into the trigger, Bahru suddenly steps back from the podium to allow for another round of loud applause from the crowd.

Jarret reels, having come so close.

Bahru then steps up to the podium and back into Jarret's sites, to finish his brief speech. As he does, Jarret again clenches, ready to fire, only to watch Bahru step back yet again, out of his sites, apparently through with his speech. As Bahru waves goodbye to the crowd, Jarret hustles to line up his shot one last time, only to hear the crack of another rifle's shot ring out from behind him.

Through his scope, he sees Bahru stagger backward, struck in the throat by another sniper's bullet.

As aides rush to Bahru, Jarret whips around to see the silhouetted shadow of a man and rifle, perched on the roof behind his, obscured by the sun, but apparently now tilting his rifle toward Jarret.

Jarret instantly rolls away as the sniper's bullet explodes into the roof where he just lay. As he curls up behind the air duct, now visible from below, the crowd begins to point up at him, screaming to the police, crying out for his capture.

He then sees the sniper retreating, heading back into the neighboring roof's access door.

So Jarret takes off, too, determined to trap the sniper in the adjacent building before he can escape, just as all hell breaks loose in the square below.

A wave of Bahru's supporters, determined to get to Jarret, charge the police lines, clashing with the officers who beat them back with batons.

But a second surge of protestors break through the police and crash into the building's lobby, allowing a mob of hell-bent Bahru supporters to bound up the stairs, determined to mete out justice with their bare hands.

Jarret, rushing down the stairs, hears their angry voices echoing up from below, and he slips out a third-story window ledge just as the mob rush past him, bounding up the stairs.

Realizing his only escape now is to jump, he sees an old truck laden with produce, speeding down the alleyway between the two buildings, trying to escape the chaos.

So just as one of the protesters spots him on the ledge and calls to his comrades, Jarret leaps, crashing down into the truck's cargo of vegetables to bounce out its back and tumble onto the pavement, jamming and spraining his ankle as he does.

As intense pain shoots up his leg, all but incapacitating him, he nevertheless climbs back to his feet and hobbles into the next building over, the sniper's building.

Finding his way into its empty lobby, he hears a door bang, and limps towards the sound, turning a corner to see an emergency exit door ajar.

So he hobbles out it to see the sniper disappearing into the rioting crowds. He's about to rush after him but then thinks better and looks around for something with which to disguise himself.

Now wearing a stolen baseball cap and tourist T-shirt, he limps back into the rioting square where tear gas immediately burns into his eyes. He then sees the water canon trucks arriving, shooting their powerful sprays, driving some rioters back while others throw rocks or retrieve the skittering, smoke-belching tear gas canisters to heave back at the police.

As he looks quickly around, determining which direction to go, a bullet explodes into the pavement by his foot.

Instantly recognizing he's under fire, he zigzags away into the chaos, taking cover behind a tree to spot the sniper's position, only to have a second shot graze his shoulder, knocking him down.

But he scrambles back to his feet and hobbles for cover again, this time using a passing water-canon truck, keeping pace with it just far enough for him to slip down a side street, escaping the square and the sniper's view, only to find himself fighting his way through a new surge of protesters streaming through the marketplace, taking up arms against the rush of police.

Jarret is pushed and shoved as he fights his way to a burning, over-turned vendor's cart, where he hides and takes out his cell phone to call

Helen, only to hear a recording explain that the number's no longer in service.

Jarret's face galvanizes as he comes to the inevitable conclusion.

Limping, bleeding from his hand and shot-grazed shoulder, he hurries up to Dalang and Lia's door and bangs on it. No one answers, so he bangs again, causing the door to creak open, and he charges in to find the place has been ransacked. As he hobbles warily through the disarray, Lia suddenly steps into view.

He gasps with relief.

Oh thank god!

As he starts toward her, she raises a gun, halting him; her eyes are burning at him, and it dawns on him what she must think.

I didn't do it. It wasn't me.

My father's dead.

Jarret grimaces, stung.

Bahru's dead.

She cocks the gun, fingering its trigger.

It wasn't me.

No? Isn't that why you came here? Isn't that what you are?

It was. It is. But I...didn't do it. I swear. The only reason I went was to keep you safe.

You mean to kill me, don't you?

No! I swear! They want me dead, too.

Why, of all people, would they want you dead?

Because...

A simple realization fills his face.

Because I'm the fall guy.

Whose?

General Matak's.

As anguished tears stream down her face, she keeps the gun on him. But her hands begin to tremble as he stands there, not fighting, not resisting, but relenting, succumbing, even welcoming this moment.

It's okay.

Lia tries hard to kill him—fighting with herself—staring down the barrel of the gun at him, ready to shoot. Wanting to shoot.

And for a moment, time seems to slow—Lia poised to shoot, Jarret ready to receive her bullet like a blessing—until she suddenly drops the gun and sinks to her knees, sobbing.

He eyes her, his soul spinning as if swimming back from a great distance as he moves her and kneels to comfort her. But when she looks at him, her eyes full of a pain beyond words, he knows there can be no comfort.

My father's dead.

Her knees give way, and she sinks to the floor.

I'm so sorry.

The police found the cars and set fire to our safe house. When we tried to escape, they shot him.

You're not going to die here, understand? You're not!

He lifts her helpless frame, and walks her out, taking the gun with him.

They emerge again into the chaos of the marketplace, the smoke and burning tires, and the bursts of gunfire ringing out through the city.

But within only a few steps, another sniper's shot rips the air, missing them by only inches as it explodes into the pavement.

Shit!

He shoves Lia behind the stucco wall, and they're forced to crawl for cover, searching for safety as more shots explode into the wall, pock-marking it.

Is this who killed Bahru?

Jarret nods, and suddenly takes out his phone, shaking his head. Lia watches him, confused.

What?

This is how they tracked me. The whole time.

Another bullet bursts just above them and they cringe away as it scatters tiny wall-fragments over them.

I'm going to make a run for it. When I do, I want you to count to twenty and go that way. Back to the hotel room as fast as you can. I'll meet you there. All right?

She nods and Jarret rushes off, instantly drawing more fire as he dodges in and out of the booths, hobbling back into the marketplace with his phone, the homing device, in hand.

Emerging from his hiding place behind a booth, Rafa takes off after Jarret, blood in his eyes, relishing the chase.

Checking his smartphone, Rafa quickly picks up Jarret's heading and runs after him just as Lia completes her count and runs off in the opposite direction.

As Jarret moves off into the streets, dodging the skirmishes and frantic rushes of protestors escaping the police, he makes his way out of the marketplace and peels off toward the public park, heading for the Buddha shrine.

Rafa follows, freed from the shadows, freed to now humiliate his nemesis before killing him.

Arriving at the serene stone Buddha, Jarret disappears behind it. Rafa, close on his heels, arrives a moment later to find everything still.

As the city's riots echo in the distance, Rafa checks his smartphone again and, locating the precise position of Jarret on it, begins the final leg of his hunt, grinning, sensing that the moment for which he's waited is finally here.

He readies his rifle and eases up on Jarret's position, quickly locating, through the overhanging leaves, Jarret's back.

As Rafa takes careful aim, savoring every second, he hears a click behind him, shocking him, turning his face to ash.

Maybe you should have stuck to stationary targets.

Rafa carefully lays the rifle down and slowly glances back to find Jarret, jacket-less, training the handgun at his head.

I had to, brah. She forced me. Just like she forced you. Hell, she told she'd make sure I'd never leave here alive if I didn't.

Really?

I swear to god, brah. Why didn't you warn me about her?

Warn you?

About who she really is. What she is.

Which is what, a killer? Like you? Like me? What'd you think she was?

Rafa can't think of a good answer.

I don't know, but…just please don't kill me. I know we can work this out.

Work what out?

Hey, I made a mistake, okay! I was scared and I made a mistake.

In that case . . .

Jarret fires two quick shots into each of Rafa's hands, shattering them.

Rafa cries out in pain and then curls up, gritting his teeth against the intense agony radiating up from his destroyed appendages.

It was them, or you.

Rafa begins to hyperventilate, shaking, his hands little more than bloody stumps now.

Why didn't you just kill me, brah?

If this doesn't work, and stop you from doing what you do, I will. Understand?

Rafa's eyes burn up at him like he's crazy.

Come on, let's get you to a hospital.

He helps Rafa to his feet and all but carries him away.

Helen, meanwhile, is pacing, awaiting word. She pauses to peer out her hotel room's window, concerned by the rioting in the streets and worried by the lack of news from Rafa. As she checks her watch, a knock on her door seems to answer her worries, and she hurries to it, unlocks and flings it open to find Jarret.

She blanches backwards in shock, withering as Jarret enters and closes the door behind him and then backs her into the room's bed, where she tries one last time.

Is it all taken care of, babe?

He smirks, cutting through her bluff, ending the charade.

If you mean Rafa, yes. He's taken care of. Now all that's left is you.

She sobers, forced to terms.

Always you were the best, babe.

That why you wanted me dead?

That was different.

Different?

He keeps moving toward her until she falls back onto the bed.

Different how?

Different like an unbelievably stupid mistake.

So in spite of all your talk about it being you who was in danger, turns out I was the fall guy.

If Rafa hadn't done what he did, they'd be comin for me, sweetie.

You mean General Matak's guys?

Helen starts to break down.

Yes.

And they probably paid you a lot of money, too.

It wasn't my idea, okay? It was just they insisted!

On what?

That whoever did it needed to go, too.

He eyes her, amazed.

It was a lot of money. A lot.

I understand. Now turn over.

She turns over, turning ashen as she does, terrified that he's positioning her for execution.

You would have done the same thing. Hell, what am I saying, you've done the same thing for the last twenty years.

You're right.

I mean, put yourself in my position, darlin'.

He presses the gun into the back of her head.

You mean face down on some strange bed with a gun to the back of your head?

Is this really?

Goodbye, Helen.

Come on, babe, you've won! To the victor go the spoils. And it's all right there, just waitin' there for ya.

She indicates, and Jarret looks over to see a black briefcase, just like the one shown earlier with all that cash.

Take it. All of it. It's yours.

He then starts to see the murky hues of her aura, like fumes, emanating shadows from her head and heart.

Please take it!

Sobering, he presses the barrel of the gun into the back of her head.

As she gasps, sure her moment has come, he leans in and whispers:

How's it feel?

Bad, baby. Real bad.

He then cocks the gun as she whimpers, squeezing her eyes shut, unable to breathe, when…click.

She lies there, frozen, only to suddenly realize she's not dead. At which she breaks down into sobs.

You're going to retire, Helen. Understood?

She gasps again, nodding, unable to speak through her sobs.

And just so we're clear, if you ever, ever come out of retirement, I will find you, Helen. Understand?

She nods again, still struggling to breathe as a minute ticks past and she suddenly realizes he hasn't said anything.

Jarret?

No answer.

Baby?

She turns ever-so-gingerly to discover he's gone.

He makes his way back to his hotel, the black briefcase tucked under his arm as he moves past burning tires, billowing up asphyxiating gushers of soot as sirens wail and gunfire echo in the black, tear-gas tinged air.

Finding his hotel bolted shut against looters, Jarret makes his way around to his room's window and climbs in with Lia's help. Though she had been desperate to see him, she now looks on confused as he presses the briefcase into her hands.

For you. Stay here, okay?

Where are you going?!

To find Daksa.

He then opens it, pulls out a few stacks of cash, and hugs her.

Stuffing the cash into his jacket, he climbs out and, dodging a protestor's skirmish with the police, steals away through the riot-torn streets, angling back toward Daksa's abode under the bridge.

He arrives to find Daksa huddling, hiding, too scared to move.

You okay?

Daksa nods, confused why he's come.

I have something for you.

He pulls out the money, and pushes into Daksa's hands.

Now go somewhere safe, okay?

Daksa eyes the cash, astonished, dumbfounded.

Go. Now.

Daksa lunges at Jarret, hugs him with a furtive smile, scrambles to his feet and runs away, escaping into the slums.

Jarret watches after him, feeling a peace coming over, and contentment, as he crawls out from under the bridge and climbs back up to the street, eager now to be with Lia, to protect and take care of her. But just as he starts back, something slams into his side like a hammer, staggering him.

He lurches forward in shock, the world beginning to spin before him as he turns to see Sergeant Tre, a few feet away, training a gun, glaring victoriously.

As Jarret crumples to his knees, Tre fires another shot into his chest, knocking him to the ground.

Tre sneers, his vengeance delivered, and turns to go, only to see a rush of rioters stumbling upon him. They instantly recognize him and charge after him. Tre tries to run, to escape, firing at them, but they quickly overtake him and throw him to the ground, driving their fists into him.

Jarret's vision grows dimmer and everything seems to slow down and down, until the rioters seem rather like Wayang puppets, their fiery auras undulating like watercolors, their elongated shapes rising and falling in the clouds of smoke, dancing, dancing, dancing the world into shadows.

With the last of his strength, he turns his face to the sky and, seeing the gray clouds drifting in the infinite sweep of the heavens, he closes his eyes, shedding one by one the wounds, fears, and terrors that had held him prisoner, held the boy in him hostage, isolating him, blinding him, breaking him, but now fading away into the ether as a city burns in the distance, a crowd riots, and the wordless, dreamless voice of silence calls to him at last, releasing him finally from the shadow-light of a fleeting world now…gone.

A gentle morning mist.

A lush, tropical hillside.

A woman mediating on a precipice.

Lia is seated on a small perch overlooking a deep, verdant valley. Her legs are folded in a lotus position, her attention turned wholly inward, as the sun, looking now like an opalescent moon floating in the mists, rises slowly in the East. A distant windchime echoes with the song of a wandering breeze as it makes it way up to her perch, brushing against her skin and hair as a lark sings in the valley, as if calling her back.

She exhales, rising from the depths, slowly surfacing again into the present as Daksa, climbing up to her perch from a footpath below, slows to make sure he's not disturbing her. But seeing her stretch, he approaches.

Your patients are here, ma'am.

She turns to him, revealing her pregnant belly, six months with child. She nods, still finding her way back into this world and then gets up to join him.

They walk along the footpath through low hanging trees and banana leaves, arriving at a clearing to find three, newly-built thatched-roof dwellings.

They pause as if they still can't quite believe their eyes.

After the rainy season, we'll build the infirmary there.

She indicates, and he nods, seeing it in his mind. They share a knowing look before moving on.

Inside her office, a small, worried woman with world-weary eyes holds up her pale baby girl.

My daughter, she very sick, ma'am.

...Only on this side.
This side?
Lia's numinous gaze smiles with compassion.
This side of the sky.
As the woman looks on, lost but grateful, Lia sobers, her face filling with light and shadows as she cups the wan girl's little cheeks in her warm palms.
You'll see, dear...you'll see.

~*~

Author

Raised in Los Angeles, Darryl Sollerh's recent works include his award winning novellas "EDDY FALLS", "ALIBIS OF THE HEART", "MINDFALL", "TRANCER" and "COWBOY AND INDIAN", a recent Readers' Favorite SILVER MEDAL BOOK AWARD winner. All are available in print, or on Kindle. For more, visit www.DarrylSollerh.com

In loving memory of
Alba Elanor Losey Dilts

~*~